THE ADVENTURES
of
BUBBA JONES

TIME-TRAVELING THROUGH SHENANDOAH NATIONAL PARK

The Adventures of Bubba Jones is a Trademark (TM) of Jeff Alt

Library of Congress Cataloging-in-Publication Data On File

ISBN
9780825308314

For inquiries about volume orders, please contact:
Beaufort Books
27 West 20th Street, Suite 1102
New York, NY 10011
sales@beaufortbooks.com

Published in the United States by Beaufort Books
www.beaufortbooks.com

Distributed by Midpoint Trade Books
www.midpointtrade.com

Printed in the United States of America

Interior design by Jamie Kerry of Belle Étoile Studios
Cover design and illustrations by Hannah Tuohy

A NATIONAL PARK SERIES

The Adventures
of
Bubba Jones

Time-Traveling Through Shenandoah National Park

BY **Jeff Alt**

WITH ILLUSTRATIONS BY Hannah Tuohy

BEAUFORT
BOOKS

BEAUFORT BOOKS
NEW YORK

DISCLAIMER

The Adventures of Bubba Jones is a piece of fiction. All the characters in this book are purely fictional, but the historical and scientific facts about Shenandoah National Park are true and accurate. The maps are not true to scale. The author has spent over eighteen years exploring Shenandoah National Park and used his wealth of park facts to create this book. Many additional sources were used to verify accuracy in the creation of this adventure, listed in the bibliography.

Dedicated to Madison & William, two great adventurers.

ACKNOWLEDGEMENTS

I would like to thank the entire Beaufort Books publishing team, especially Eric Kampmann, Megan Trank, Michael Short, and Felicia Minerva for assembling *The Adventures of Bubba Jones* into this book and getting it into the hands of those seeking an entertaining and informative adventure. I would also like to thank the following people who were instrumental in the publication of this book: Hannah Tuohy, my illustrator, for her talents in bringing my characters to life; Liz Osborn for her editorial guidance; Bill Deitzer for his historical advice; and Paul Krupin for his publicity expertise. I would like to thank the staff from Shenandoah National Park for providing information and resources, reviewing my manuscript for accuracy, and providing advice, especially: Greta Miller, Executive Director, Shenandoah National Park Association; Tim Taglauer, Park Ranger, Interpretation and Education Division, Shenandoah National Park; Claire Comer, Interpretive Specialist, Shenandoah National Park; Sally Hurlbert, Park Ranger, Interpretation and Education Division, Shenandoah National Park; Meredith McDonald Evans, Park Ranger, Interpretation and Education Division, Shenandoah National Park; and Kandace Muller, Museum Specialist, Shenandoah National Park. I would like to thank Brian King, Publisher,

The Appalachian Trail Conservancy, for providing historical verification of Appalachian Trail facts. I would like to thank Jennifer Wilcox, Museum Administrator & Educational Coordinator, National Cryptologic Museum, National Security Agency, for advising me on a secret code appropriate for the young readers of this book. And lastly, I would like to thank my wife and children and all of my family and friends that have explored Shenandoah National Park with me over the years, which helped me develop this book.

CONTENTS

IS THIS SHENANDOAH NATIONAL PARK?

T ree branches crunched and snapped from the weight of something big moving through the forest. The sound was growing louder with each passing second, and whatever was making it was moving right toward us. We crouched down close together around my sleeping sister to hide from view. No one said a word, for fear of giving away our location, but I could hear my heart beating rapidly.

The large unknown creature was so heavy it shook the ground with each step, which woke my sister. She sat up and looked around in confusion as she tried to figure out where she was. When she had dozed off, she was comfortably seated in the back seat of our Jeep as we traveled down the highway en route to Shenandoah National Park; now she was sitting in the middle of the woods with no vehicle in sight and an unknown beast approaching us. Turning to look at us, she saw that we were dressed in animal hides, like prehistoric people. She looked down at herself, and looked even more confused at seeing that she, too, was dressed in animal skin.

An unusually cool breeze blew through the forest, causing us to shiver. We huddled closer together for warmth. This did not feel like the same Shenandoah National Park, a place that draws over 1.2 million visitors annually, that Papa Lewis had described to us. Our grandfather, Papa Lewis, named after the famed Meriwether Lewis of the Lewis and Clark expedition, had explored Shenandoah National Park on many adventures and had shared all of his exciting stories with us. Whenever he talked about Shenandoah, he had a twinkle in his eyes and a smile on his face that let us know how special the park was to him. After hearing him describe it, we couldn't wait to explore it ourselves!

The sound of snapping twigs and branches grew louder. Whatever this beast was, it was getting closer to us. Small trees swayed nearby as this animal easily pushed through them. *Whatever it is, it's big,* I thought to myself. *Can it smell us? Does it know we're here?* A jolt of fear shot down my spine and a lump formed in my throat.

"Where are we?" Hug-a-Bug asked. Hug-a-Bug is my sister. Her real name is Jenny, but we call her Hug-a-Bug for her love of everything outdoors.

"We're at Rockfish Gap, near the south entrance of Shenandoah National Park," I whispered.

Hug-a-Bug knew from Papa Lewis that if we were at Rockfish Gap entering Shenandoah National Park, then we should be either hiking on the Appalachian Trail or driving on Skyline Drive. Papa Lewis had told us all about Skyline Drive, a road that rambles along the top of the mountain from Rockfish Gap, Virginia for a hundred and five miles, all the way up to Front Royal, Virginia. He had also described countless hikes along the Appalachian Trail, which follows alongside Skyline Drive through the entire length of Shenandoah National Park. I watched as my sister scanned the landscape for signs of the trail or the road. Finding neither, she looked even more confused. She looked down at her clothing again.

"What am I wearing?"

"It looks like a buffalo skin to me," I replied casually, as if that was nothing out of the ordinary.

"Shhh! Stay quiet everyone! We don't want to draw attention from whatever is making the noise," Papa Lewis whispered as we remained huddled in a stand of trees.

Tree limbs cracked just inches from us. Dad, also known as Clark, after the famous Lewis and Clark duo, picked up a large rock to possibly throw at the unknown creature. Whatever was moving through the forest was literally almost right on top of us. We all sat still and quiet, wondering *what next?* You could have heard a pin drop.

Suddenly, the tree branches shook above us and a massive head appeared. At first I thought it was an elephant, but then I noticed its tusks were thicker and longer than any I had ever seen before. Its ears were relatively small, not at all like an elephant's. And it was furry!! If it took one more step, its enormous foot would crush us! Unable to take the waiting in silence any longer, Hug-a-Bug stood up and slowly backed away from the beast. Now, backing away slowly is recommended in black bear encounters if you get too close, but this creature was no black bear!

Fortunately, however, Hug-a-Bug's movement seemed to frighten the animal because it turned and thundered off into the forest. The sounds of snapping tree branches faded as the beast plowed through the trees and disappeared.

"Wh—what was that?" Hug-a-Bug asked, trembling with fear.

"That was a woolly mammoth, an ancient cousin of the elephant. Woolly mammoths and mastodons lived in this area until they became extinct about 10,000 years ago. They began to die off as the glaciers retreated at the end of the Ice Age and the climate warmed up. Right now there are still glaciers within a few hundred miles of the area, which explains the cooler temperatures. Woolly mammoth and mastodon bones have been found in the valleys near the present-day Shenandoah National Park. These huge creatures were herbivores and didn't eat meat, so we were safe from being its next meal. But I'm guessing that some kind of carnivorous predator chased it up here from the valley, hoping for one huge slab of mammoth steak for dinner. Since it didn't get the mammoth, it might come looking for other prey, and that includes us," Papa Lewis explained in a hushed tone.

"I'm confused. Let me get this straight. Are you saying that we just came face to face with a woolly mammoth that went extinct 10,000 years ago? How could that …"

I cut my sister off in mid-sentence and blurted, "What sort of predator are you talking about?!"

"Well, based on the animal skin we're wearing, the prehistoric Paleo-Indians are here and they might be trying to hunt that woolly mammoth for food. It could also be other predators like a mountain lion or..."

Before Papa Lewis could complete his explanation something flew by us with a *whoosh* followed by a *thunk*. Instinctively we dropped, flattening ourselves to the ground. About the same time we hit the ground, so did a primitive-looking spear. That explained the whoosh and the thunk—a spear had sailed by us, glanced off a tree, then fallen to the ground just a short distance from us.

"Quiet! No one move!" Papa Lewis hissed.

We heard voices coming from the brush, but I couldn't make out what they were saying. As we watched, holding our breath, the branches on a nearby bush shook, then were pushed aside as a figure emerged. Near as I could tell, he was some sort of Indian. He had coarse black hair and was clothed in animal skin. He was soon followed by three other men of similar appearance. They walked within a few feet of us, scanning the nearby trees and searching through the grass. It looked like they were trying to find the spear they threw. Time slowed to a snail's pace as we lay motionless in the brush, hoping to go undetected. I scrunched my eyes shut in fear, and, while hearing the men talking again, realized the reason I couldn't make out what they were saying was because they weren't speaking English. A few more moments passed when I heard more rustling, followed by more talking. Opening one eye to see what was going on, I saw the hunters regroup and move on, apparently giving up the hunt for their spear. They followed the path of broken tree limbs and tracks left by the woolly mammoth, and soon disappeared from view.

"Man, that was close!" I breathed.

"Don't they know hunting is not allowed in Shenandoah National park?" Hug-a-Bug demanded.

"I don't think this is a national park yet," Papa Lewis reminded her.

"I'm confused. If we're not in a national park, then shouldn't we be wearing orange during hunting season so the hunters know we're not game?"

"Yes, normally orange is recommended, but, we're in an unusual situation right now," Papa Lewis explained.

We all stood up and Papa Lewis walked over to the spear that lay beneath the tree it had struck. He picked it up and examined it.

"Look what we have here," Papa Lewis said holding out the spear in front of him and pointing at the tip. A long stone arrow was tied to the end of the stick. The arrow was about three inches long. It was slightly oval in shape and came to a sharp point at the very tip.

"This is a Clovis point. The first humans to live in this area, the nomadic Paleo Indians, used this to penetrate the thick skin of big animals. It looks like those men were hunting the woolly mammoth and when they saw movement through the trees, they mistook us for him! Archeologists have found these Clovis points in the area. Scientists have also found evidence that suggests that the Paleo Indians, the woolly mammoths, and the mastodons coexisted until the elephant-like creatures became extinct. The scientists suspect that the early Paleo Indians tried their best at hunting the last remaining woolly mammoths and mastodons, but they probably had better luck hunting buffalo, elk, and deer. I would say by what we just witnessed, their suspicions are correct," Papa Lewis explained.

"You said the Paleo Indians were nomadic. What does nomadic mean?" Hug-a-Bug asked Papa Lewis.

"Nomadic means they traveled and didn't stay in one place. They followed the wild animals that they hunted for food." Papa Lewis answered.

"I hope they don't hurt that wooly mammoth. It didn't want to hurt anyone. It was actually afraid of us," Hug-a-Bug said, "But anyway, enough of the history lesson, back to the present. What happened here? I fall asleep in our Jeep on the way to Shenandoah National Park, I wake up and almost get stepped on by a creature that went extinct 10,000 years ago, we almost get speared by prehistoric hunters, our Jeep is nowhere in sight, and I'm now wearing dead animal skin, and Skyline Drive and the Appalachian Trail have apparently not even been built yet. Bubba Jones, did you do what I think you did?!"

ACTION AT ROCKFISH GAP

"Did you take us on a time travel adventure while I was sleeping?!" Hug-a-Bug demanded.

My real name is Tommy, but everyone calls me Bubba Jones for my sense of adventure.

What I'm about to tell you, I still have a hard time believing myself. If you followed us on our first adventure, then you already know. But here it is: I have the ability to travel back in time. Hug-a-Bug will soon have that ability as well. We inherited this amazing skill from our grandfather, Papa Lewis, on our last adventure. Our family's legendary time travel skill goes all the way back to the time of the Lewis and Clark expedition. When Meriwether Lewis and William Clark returned from their Corps of Discovery expedition, our ancestors realized that the pristine wildlands Lewis and Clark explored were at risk of vanishing without careful preservation. Many people would soon head west. New cities and towns would take root and the untouched wilderness that Lewis and Clark explored would soon be gone forever. Our ancestors made it their mission to use their legendary time travel skills to help conserve and protect some of the wilderness areas so that future generations could enjoy them. Not only that, but they hoped their efforts would help preserve as much of the natural world as possible. And so it went; our ancestors dispersed throughout the U.S. to all wilderness areas with the mission of protecting Mother Nature in all of her glory for future generations. This all happened long before the creation of the National Park Service and National Forest Service, which now have similar goals.

Our family's time travel skills came with a strict set of rules. The time travel skills must be passed on to a relative every forty years. It is recommended to skip a generation and pass on the legendary skills only to a family member who is capable of exploring America's wildlands, and willing to inherit the magic, as well as the responsibility that comes with it. Hug-a-Bug and I agreed to accept this skill from our Papa Lewis. How could we refuse? Going back and actually watching history unfold is amazing!! Way better than learning about it in Mrs. Gruber's class!

"Yes, Hug-a-Bug, I took us back in time. I was just so excited about our Shenandoah National Park adventure, and I was curious what the area was like thousands of years ago. When you fell asleep, I got bored sitting in the car. It was a long drive. When we turned off the interstate and climbed up the mountain to the Rockfish Gap entrance of Shenandoah National Park, I decided to time travel back 11,000 years to see what it was like," I said.

"Bubba Jones, that's not fair to time travel without me knowing where we're going," Hug-a-Bug stated.

"Bubba Jones, I may not have covered this when I handed over the time travel skills to you, but for safety, everyone you time travel with should be awake and aware of the time period to which you are traveling. It's also smart to know what to expect before you time travel," Papa Lewis stated.

"That totally makes sense now. This time travel is serious business. I won't do it again," I responded.

I'm still getting the hang of this amazing ability I just inherited from Papa Lewis, and I'm sure glad he's traveling with us. I don't even want to think of what might have happened if he wasn't! Papa Lewis knows all the ins and outs of time travel. He had this ability for forty years before handing it over to me. He has also explored nearly every wild place in the country and he absorbs every fact about each area he explores. He's a walking encyclopedia. He knew that was a wooly mammoth. He knew those were prehistoric Paleo Indians. He knew what a Clovis point was.

Mom, affectionately known as Petunia, said what we all were thinking: "Bubba Jones, take us back to the present!"

This was a very wild place and time in human history. Who knew what would happen next?! When Papa Lewis handed over the time travel skill to me, he gave me the family journal, an old leather-bound book, that has family recordings dating back to the Revolutionary War. Not only is the journal filled with our family history, it is also the source of my time travel ability— I have to have the journal with me to time travel. There are other rules as well: We can only visit the past, not the future. Anyone can time travel with me as long as they are within ten feet of me at the moment of departure. And we need to be near the location to which we want to time travel.

Everyone eagerly waited as I said, "Take us back to the present."

I felt a gust of warm air and seconds later we were back in the Jeep, buckled in and bouncing along the road. The animal skins were gone, replaced by our T-shirts and shorts. I never thought I would enjoy being in the back seat of a car after such a long drive, but now I sure was! We all were! Papa Lewis was driving and following a line of cars, trucks, RVs, motorcycles, and bicycles on a two-lane road. A sign on the side of the road read "Shenandoah National Park" with an arrow pointing north and "Blue Ridge Parkway" with an arrow pointing south. The road we were on ran along on the top of a mountain ridge. We could see farm fields and a forested valley below. The line of traffic snaked northward around a bend and disappeared from view into the park.

"Now this looks like the entrance to Shenandoah National Park that Papa Lewis told us about," Hug-a-Bug said with a smile.

"That's right, Hug-a-Bug. We're at the southern tip of Shenandoah National Park, a junction where the Blue Ridge Parkway connects to Skyline Drive. As soon as we clear the Rockfish Gap entrance station, we will officially be in the park," Papa Lewis replied cheerfully. He added, "Rockfish Gap is rich with history. This gap is one of only a few low-lying gaps in Shenandoah National Park region, making it one of the easier places to cross over the mountains if you're traveling east or west. Herds of buffalo have passed through here, Indians, settlers, armies, and as you've witnessed, woolly mammoths. Thomas Jefferson, the third president of the United States and the man who wrote the Declaration of Independence, held a meeting right here in 1818 to decide where to build the University of Virginia."

"Bubba Jones, if you had given me a choice between dodging spears and almost being stepped on by a prehistoric elephant or meeting President Thomas Jefferson, I would've picked meeting the president hands down. Just saying," Hug-a-Bug stated.

"But Hug-a-Bug, how many people do you know that have come face-to-face with a woolly mammoth and prehistoric nomadic Indians?" I replied.

"We've certainly had quite a taste of adventure, and our Shenandoah expedition has only just begun!" Papa Lewis stated matter-of-factly.

"Yep, but how about that meeting with Thomas Jefferson? We're right here. If we don't go back and meet him, that would be like letting your favorite ice cream melt instead of eating it," Hug-a-Bug insisted.

"You got it, Hug-a-Bug. No one wants to waste good ice cream!" I responded with a grin. We all laughed.

"Bubba Jones, take us back to August 4, 1818," Papa Lewis suggested.

I placed my hand on the family journal and repeated the exact date Papa Lewis had said. A gust of wind smacked us and a few seconds later our seat belts vanished along with the Jeep. We now sat in an open-top horse-drawn carriage. Hug-a-Bug, Grandma, and Mom wore long dresses down to their ankles and veils on their heads, adorned with fresh flowers. Papa Lewis, Dad, and I all had on skin-tight breeches, tall boots, overcoats cropped at the waist but with long tails in the back, and top hats. Our shirts had ruffles spilling down the front. It was a hot summer day, and these clothes seemed a little much for the weather. We were parked in front of a log building. A sign hung from the porch that read "Mountain Top Tavern." At least thirty horses and carriages were parked all around the tavern, with the horses' reins tied to posts.

Hug-a-Bug sat directly across from me in the carriage. She held an open umbrella over her head.

"Hug-a-Bug, do you know that you have an umbrella and it's not raining?" I asked with a laugh.

Before Hug-a-Bug had a chance to answer, Papa Lewis responded, "Bubba Jones, in this time period, that kind of umbrella was called a parasol. Ladies used it to shade their face from the sun. But back to the business at hand. Right now, there are three former presidents and twenty-four delegates meeting inside that tavern," Papa Lewis said, pointing to the log building in front of us.

"They are meeting to decide where to build the University of Virginia. Let's go in and join them," Papa Lewis suggested.

He hopped down from the driver's seat of the carriage and wrapped the horse's reins around a post in the yard. We all stepped down from the carriage and followed Papa Lewis towards the tavern porch. Before we reached the steps, the front door swung open and men began exiting the building, spilling onto the porch. They were all wearing the same type of clothing as us. As the men filed out, they shook hands, patted each other on the back and dispersed toward their respective horses and carriages. Three men remained on the porch talking.

"That's President Jefferson and he's talking to two other former presidents, James Madison and James Monroe," Papa Lewis whispered as we ascended the porch steps.

Hug-a-Bug walked over to Thomas Jefferson and stood next to him. The rest of us stood nearby on the porch. Hug-a-Bug had a smile from ear to ear. She just stood there and gazed in awe at President Jefferson. I pulled a nickel out of my pocket and compared Jefferson's image on the coin to the actual man. *Pretty close*, I thought. President Jefferson shook hands with James Madison and James Monroe, bringing a close to their conversation. Mr. Madison and Mr. Monroe stepped off the porch and climbed up into their respective horse-drawn carriages and drove off down a narrow lane. My sister's presence had piqued Mr. Jefferson's curiosity.

"Who might you be, young lady?" President Jefferson asked, looking down at Hug-a-Bug.

"I'm Hug-a-Bug, Mr. President, and I wanted to meet you," Hug-a-Bug said.

"Well it's nice to meet you, Hug-a-Bug. What an interesting name you have. You traveled all the way up here just to meet me?" Mr. Jefferson asked.

"Well, not quite. My family and I are going to explore the area, and I heard you were up here on the mountain for a meeting," Hug-a-Bug explained. (She was careful not to use the word "Shenandoah" because the park hadn't been created and named yet).

"I'm impressed that you're interested in exploring the wilderness. What a great way to discover the world around you! I'm a big supporter of exploration. I dispatched Lewis and Clark on the Corps of Discovery to explore the western wilderness while I was president.

"It sure feels good to be outside in this fresh air. We sat in that tavern all day to decide where to build the University of Virginia. I'm pleased to say that we agreed to make Charlottesville, Virginia, my home town, the location. Those who study there will have a beautiful view of the mountains you're about to explore. Nice to meet you, Hug-a-Bug," former President Jefferson said, taking her hand in both of his and bowing slightly. Then he turned and stepped off the porch, climbed into his carriage, and drove off down a narrow dirt road. Hug-a-Bug stood there smiling and speechless, and watched President Jefferson until his horse and buggy became a mere speck in the distance with nothing but a swirl of road dust left behind.

"Let's get on with our Shenandoah adventure," Papa Lewis suggested as he stepped off the porch and walked back towards our carriage.

We all followed him and climbed back into our carriage seats. I placed my hand on the family journal tucked into my pocket and said, "Take us back to the present."

A gust of hot air blasted us. The carriage jolted up and down. Seconds later, we were all seated back in our Jeep moving in a line of traffic towards the park entrance. It was nice to wear shorts and a T-shirt again.

"That was awesome! I got to meet President Jefferson—the author of the Declaration of Independence! There sure are a lot of famous people that visited Rockfish Gap," Hug-a-Bug said

"Back then, most people lived in Virginia and the other colonial states along the east coast. It wasn't until after the Lewis and Clark expedition that people began to move west," Papa Lewis explained.

"So this was where all the action happened?" I asked.

"You could say that."

I could feel the energy and excitement in the air, knowing we were about to enter Shenandoah National Park. We had already had quite an adventure right here at the Rockfish Gap entrance, and it fueled our excitement as to what we would discover inside the park itself. Papa Lewis had shared so many tales from his own Shenandoah exploits, we couldn't wait to finally experience the park with him!

We're actually a year ahead of our originally planned Shenandoah National Park adventure. Something happened that abruptly changed our plans. You see, not only did Hug-a-Bug and I inherit Papa Lewis' time traveling skills; we also took over an unsolved mystery, and we had discovered a clue that led us to Shenandoah National Park. So here we are, a year ahead of schedule and on the trail of a clue.

CHAPTER 3

SECRET IN THE MAIL

Sandwiched between the pages of the family journal that Papa Lewis had passed along to me was an old, tattered half-sheet of paper with some sort of code written on it. Papa Lewis had never figured out what it meant. The paper was torn almost exactly in half, so we figured that the other half of the page had the rest of the coded message. On our first adventure, in the Smokies, we found Papa Lewis' long-lost cousin Wild Bill in the Great Smoky Mountain National Park. Wild Bill and Papa Lewis had inherited their time-traveling ability from their grandfather while on a camping trip together forty years ago, and Wild Bill had the missing half of the paper all this time. Wild Bill gave us his half, and he turned over his time-traveling skills to our cousin Crockett. Together, we had all worked to try to crack the code.

We had some success, but it wasn't enough to decode the message. On the last day of our Great Smoky Mountain adventure, we had figured out a key phrase to use with the code: "Great National Parks." But it wasn't enough; something was missing. Crockett, Hug-a-Bug, and I had sat around our campsite picnic table for hours, but we couldn't make sense of the code. We had the two halves of paper back together. The paper was filled with a line grid of columns and rows with a letter in each box. The entire alphabet was printed across the top row of the grid, with one letter for each column. The entire alphabet was also listed again down the left column, with a letter for each row. Finally, we had put the code aside. Mom had suggested that we take a break and join everyone around the campfire for a last night of family time.

We had all cozied into our camp chairs around the fire and set up our famous s'more assembly line. Crocket and I roasted marshmallows on sticks, and Hug-a-Bug lined up graham crackers and chocolate squares up on the edge of the picnic table. In no time, we had s'mores for everyone. We all sat staring into the fire and enjoying each other's company. The next morning, everyone would go their separate ways. Aunt Walks-a-Lot, Uncle Boone, and our cousin Crocket would head back to Georgia. Wild Bill would remain in the Smokies, and we would head back to Ohio.

While we sat around the fire and talked about our adventures, Wild Bill quietly sorted through a stack of mail piled on his lap. Having been in the mountains for a while, he found his mail had piled up in his absence. Earlier in the day, he had slipped into town and retrieved it from a friend who holds his mail for him while he explores. A beam of light from the headlamp strapped to his head shone down onto his mail. Wild Bill held up an unopened envelope and said, "This is odd. I believe this letter is for Bubba Jones, Hug-a-Bug, and Crockett."

"Why would someone send you our mail?" I asked.

"We're kids; we don't get mail," Hug-a-Bug added.

I stood up and walked over to Wild Bill. He handed me a standard letter-size envelope. The last line of the address read "Attn: Keepers of our Family Heritage." The letter didn't have a return address, but it had a postmark from Washington D.C. I walked back over to my chair, sat down, turned on my headlamp, and tore open the envelope. Crockett and Hug-a-Bug crowded around me and looked over my shoulder as the light of my headlamp fell on the note. We all read the letter silently.

Dear Time Traveling Kin,

I expect that by now you have both pieces of the cipher, and you've figured out the passcode that starts with the word "great." The message requires a second code to decipher. Here it is: (LQ&MHDCVST). Use the "great" code for the alphabet across the top. Use this second code for the alphabet column that runs down the left side. Find each intersecting letter on the sheet and this will give you the location of the next national park to explore. Go there and I will meet up with you. I will see you there. Happy adventures!

"Finally, a breakthrough! We got a letter from a relative who knows all about the code we're trying to crack, and they gave us instructions on how to decipher the message," I exclaimed.

"Can I see the letter?" Papa Lewis asked.

I handed it over. He looked at it for a minute and then responded, "Remarkable! Of course! I can't believe I didn't think of this before! This coded message is a replica of the cipher system that Lewis and Clark used with President Jefferson during their Corps of Discovery Expedition. Only difference being Lewis and Clark used Artichoke as their passcode for the alphabet column across the top of the code sheet. They used a second set of nonsense letters for the row of alphabet along the left side of the code sheet. Then they would simply follow the row each nonsense letter, in order, across the grid and match it with each letter from the passcode column down from the top. The letter in the grid box will spell out your secret message. This is as simple as matching up rows and columns," Papa Lewis explained.

Pass Code: G R E A T N A T I O
(column across the top of grid)

Coded Message: L Q & M H & C V S T
(row down the left side of grid)

Crocket, Hug-a-Bug, and I walked away from the fire over to the picnic table and sat down to try to crack the code again. While we worked at deciphering the message, Papa Lewis took out an Irish flute. He held it to his mouth just like Hug-a-Bug holds her clarinet. We had never seen nor heard Papa Lewis play this instrument. But that's the way Papa Lewis is—full of mystery and surprises. He began to play a soothing melody as we continued to decipher the code. We had already deciphered the first four letters of a word, "S-H-E-N" when Wild Bill began to sing along with Papa Lewis' flute.

"O Shenandoah, I long to hear you.

Away, you rolling river

O Shenandoah, I long to hear you.

Away, I'm bound across the wide Missouri..."

Hug-a-Bug, Crocket, and I looked at each other as we heard the lyrics.

"Did you hear what I heard?? In the first verse Wild Bill sang 'Oh Shenandoah.' Shenandoah is the name of a national park," I stated.

That's weird, I thought. We finished decoding the rest of the message and it read /S-H-E-N-A-N-D-O-A-H/, the song Papa Lewis and Wild Bill were singing.

Pass Code: G R E A T N A T I O
(column across the top of grid)

Cipher Message: L Q & M H & C V S T
(row down the left side of grid)

Deciphered Message: S H E N A N D O A H
(Letters in each box found by crossing the rows and columns of the two codes above)

"'Shenandoah' is the deciphered message. The letter said to immediately go to the next park in the secret message. The mystery is solved! We need to go to Shenandoah!" I shouted excitedly.

Hug-a-Bug, Crocket, and I grabbed the coded message and marched back over to the fire. We felt that this was important enough to interrupt Papa Lewis and Wild Bill mid-song. "That's it!" I shouted, "The secret message is 'Shenandoah.' We need to go there now!" I thrust our decoded message at Papa.

"Well look at that," he said, holding his flute in one hand and the decoded letter in the other.

"Our grandpa sang 'Oh Shenandoah' to Wild Bill and me forty years ago when he turned over the time-traveling skills to us. We were just going down memory lane by singing 'Oh Shenandoah.' What a coincidence," Papa Lewis said.

Our campfire conversation changed that instant from talking about the adventure we just had in the Smokies to the next one awaiting us in Shenandoah.

"We have all the gear already packed. Instead of going home, we could head to Shenandoah. All we need is food and provisions that we can pick up on the way," Dad said.

"Clark, I like how you think. Is everyone else up for another adventure?" Papa Lewis asked.

Mom smiled and said, "Let's do it."

Grandma smiled, hugged Mom and said, "A family that goes on an adventure together learns and has fun."

Boone and Aunt-Walks-a-Lot already had work commitments back home, so they wouldn't be able to go with us. Crockett was disappointed because he really wanted to come. He was just as focused on solving our family mystery as we were. So, it was decided that he and my aunt and uncle might meet up with us later in Shenandoah. Wild Bill had some unfinished business in the Smokies that would keep him from coming along, but he said he could join us later if we needed him. He gave Papa Lewis his contact information.

The next morning we broke camp and said our good-byes. Everyone pitched in and within an hour we had the dining canopy, tents, and all our gear strapped to the top of our Jeep. Then we had a long round of goodbyes, hugging and kissing, and promising to keep in touch.

Hug-a-Bug and I assured Crockett that we would keep him in the loop on the mystery. We climbed into the Jeep, and just like that, we were on our way, headed towards Shenandoah. It felt like we were on a brand-new adventure because, well, we were!

CHAPTER 4

THE PEOPLE BEHIND THE TRAIL

The line of vehicles ahead of us moved swiftly towards the Rockfish Gap entrance to Shenandoah National Park. There are four entrances into the park. Rockfish Gap is the southernmost. We weren't quite sure how or where we would meet with the relative that sent us the passcode and led us here, but Papa Lewis told us not to worry about that.

"Whoever sent us that letter will find us. They found us in the Smokies; they will find us in Shenandoah," Papa Lewis assured us.

As we sped along, edging closer to the entrance, we passed a small parking lot on the right side of the road and Hug-a-Bug immediately took notice of three hikers. They were sitting under a small shelter, talking to tourists.

"Papa Lewis, can you pull over? Those are Appalachian Trail thru-hikers. I want to hike into the park, just like they are!" Hug-a-Bug shouted.

Papa Lewis pulled into the parking lot and shifted the Jeep into park.

"Are you sure they're thru-hikers, honey?" Mom asked Hug-a-Bug.

"Do you see the A.T. patch on their packs? The Appalachian Trail thru-hikers we met in the Smokies had the same patch. And look at the beards on them! They've been out here awhile," Hug-a-Bug pointed out.

Ever since Hug-a-Bug met Grandma Gatewood, the first woman to solo hike the Appalachian Trail, on one of our time travel adventures, Hug-a-Bug had wanted to be a thru-hiker. Grandma Gatewood had inspired her.

"If you're right, Hug-a-Bug, those hikers have walked all the way from Georgia, through Tennessee, North Carolina, and most of Virginia to get here. That's over 850 miles," Papa Lewis stated.

"Wow! But, the real way to identify a thru-hiker is the 'smell test'. The other thru-hikers we met all had an awful smell from not showering or wearing deodorant, and their synthetic clothing seems to make them smell even worse," I said.

Hug-a-Bug jumped out of the Jeep. She opened the tailgate, grabbed a sandwich from our cooler, and walked over to the hikers. Papa Lewis and I got out and followed her. Hug-a-Bug offered the hikers the sandwich, which they quickly accepted. One of the hikers tore the sandwich into three pieces and handed the other two hikers a piece, and all three inhaled it in a matter of seconds. As Hug-a-Bug chatted with them, the wind blew their scent towards where I stood and about knocked me off my feet, confirming their authenticity. I tried not to breathe through my nose. They were definitely thru-hikers! After chatting with us for a few minutes, the thru-hikers invited us to hike with them into Shenandoah National Park.

We returned to the car and Papa Lewis pulled out our hiking poles and daypacks. We hoisted our packs and reviewed a map with Dad to determine where he should meet up with us, and then we joined the thru-hikers. There are two ways adventure seekers enter Shenandoah National Park—by road or by trail— and we were about to do both. Dad pulled back out onto Skyline Drive with Mom and Grandma and drove on into the park. Papa Lewis, Hug-a-Bug, and I followed the thru-hikers along the Appalachian Trail. We officially entered the park, hiker-style. Our Shenandoah Adventure had begun!

Papa Lewis, Hug-a-Bug, and I followed the three thru-hikers northward. They were hard to keep up with. The Appalachian Trail, or A.T. for short, parallels Skyline Drive the entire length of the park for miles. Skyline Drive is 105 miles long and the A.T. has 101 miles inside the park. The thru-hikers had already covered over 800 miles of the A.T. to get to this point. They walked fast and kept in step with each other, like a finely-tuned machine. We couldn't keep their pace, and the distance between us and them grew until they were out of sight.

It was easy to know where the trail was. The A.T. was wide enough to walk side by side most of the time and every few hundred yards, the trail was marked by a white rectangle painted on a tree, letting us know we were still on the right path. The three of us stopped for a water break. Beads of sweat rolled down my cheeks and dripped off my forehead.

"Those thru-hikers are amazing. They've walked all the way from Georgia, and they walk as fast as I jog!" Hug-a-Bug said.

We continued hiking up a gradual incline. The occasional sound of a vehicle reminded us how close we were to Skyline Drive. We had made plans to meet Dad, Mom, and Grandma at Beagle Gap, a little over five miles from where they left us at Rockfish Gap. While we hiked, they drove ahead to set up our camp for the night. After a few miles, the trail came out of the woods and led us across Skyline Drive and then back onto the trail again and up a slight grade into a thicket of pine trees. I heard the sound of an axe cracking into wood. Soon we heard voices and then, rounding a bend in the trail, found the source. Six people—four men and two women—were hard at work cutting up a tree that had fallen across the trail. They all had on green t-shirts with a logo that read PATC.

"Hello, hikers! There are three hikers about twenty minutes ahead of you. They were concerned that you might be upset that they were moving faster than you," a man holding a saw called out to us.

"Hello PATC crew, thanks for all the work you're doing on the trail. We're not upset about falling behind. Those thru-hikers move like machines. We're having a nice, leisurely hike," Papa Lewis said.

"Are you the group that paints the white trail blaze marks on the trees?" Hug-a-Bug asked.

"Yep, we do that, but right now we're clearing trees that fell across the trail during the last storm. We call them blowdowns. They make it difficult for the hikers. You have to either crawl under or over them. This is nothing compared to the re-route we did last month, though. We had to move a mile of trail and move big rocks into place to prevent erosion. That took a crew of forty PATC volunteers an entire week," the PATC volunteer answered.

"What I find equally amazing as the thru-hikers who walk from Georgia to Maine are the people that built this trail and continue to take care of it. Bubba Jones and Hug-a-Bug, these folks are volunteers for the Potomac Appalachian Trail Club, or PATC. Without them, this trail might never have been made. Thank you again for all your hard work," Papa Lewis said as he continued hiking down the trail.

"Yeah, thanks," Hug-a-Bug and I said in unison and we continued on down the trail behind Papa Lewis.

"Happy trails!" the PATC volunteer hollered as the crew returned to their work.

Hug-a-Bug called out to Papa Lewis as we walked along, "I didn't realize the A.T. was man-made. I thought someone just marked a bunch of old paths that deer and Native Americans had used, and connected them all together."

"The A.T. was constructed along the spine of the Appalachian Mountain chain by people. They used existing paths when possible, but the work was very hard. They had to clear trees, move stone, build shelters, construct bridges, and post trail markers. Benton MacKaye wrote an article in 1921 that inspired the creation of the

Appalachian Trail, and the man that organized the workers to build it was Myron Avery, the first president of the PATC and seven-term chairperson of the Appalachian Trail Conservancy. Only back then they called it the Appalachian Trail Conference," Papa Lewis explained.

The trail led us out of the woods at Beagle Gap, the location where we were supposed to meet back up with Grandma, Dad, and Mom. We had hiked almost six miles, a respectable distance for anyone in mountain terrain. The Jeep wasn't there yet to pick us up, so we all took off our packs and sat down to wait in the parking area.

"Guess who the first person was to become an official Appalachian Trail 2,000- miler?" Papa Lewis asked.

"That's easy, it was Earl Shaffer in 1948," I stated confidently.

"Yes, Earl Shaffer was the first thru-hiker and Grandma Gatewood was the first female solo thru-hiker. They both walked continuously from Georgia to Maine, in one season. But Myron Avery was the first person to walk the entire trail. He did it in sections over a number of years. He completed it in 1936, before the A.T. was officially completed and twelve years before Earl Shaffer's thru-hike. Avery hiked the trail and worked with the trail crews to build it as he went," Papa Lewis explained.

"You can do that? You can walk the A.T. in sections and still be considered a 2,000-miler?" I asked.

"There is no right or wrong way to become a 2,000-miler. You just have to walk the entire A.T. You can do it in parts, or all at once. You can go from Georgia to Maine or from Maine to Georgia. You can even do a flip flop and start midway in Harpers Ferry, hike north to Maine, then catch a ride back to Harpers Ferry and hike south," Papa Lewis replied.

"Mr. Avery hiked the trail in a very cool way. I think Mr. Avery deserved to be the first 2,000-miler for all the work he did to make the trail. Maybe that's how I'll hike the A.T.: in sections," Hug-a-Bug said excitedly.

We heard an approaching vehicle on Skyline Drive and sure enough, it was our Jeep. Dad pulled into the parking lot.

"Hey guys, how was the hike?" Dad hollered from the driver's window.

"Great, Dad. We couldn't keep up with the thru-hikers, but we met a trail crew working on the A.T.," I replied.

We told him all about the PATC crew and what we learned about Myron Avery.

"Where are Grandma and Mom?" Hug-a-Bug asked.

"They're back at Loft Mountain Campground making dinner."

"Before we go, do you all mind if we time-travel back and meet Myron Avery?" I asked.

"Let's do it!" Dad said.

"Bubba Jones, take us back to the spring of 1928," Papa Lewis suggested.

Everyone circled around me as I placed my hand on the family journal and said "Take us back to the spring of 1928,"

A gust of wind smacked us and seconds later, Skyline Drive and our Jeep disappeared. Our modern synthetic clothing and hiking gear was replaced with cotton long sleeve shirts and pants, and we found ourselves carrying canvas military rucksacks like the one Papa Lewis hikes with.

"Where's Skyline Drive?" Hug-a-Bug asked.

"Skyline Drive doesn't exist yet. The Appalachian Trail in Shenandoah National Park was completed before the road was built. As a matter of fact, right now in 1928, they still don't know exactly where they will put Skyline Drive. Look around for a group of trail builders. They are working under Myron Avery's supervision. In fact, I think this is Myron Avery coming up the trail right now," Papa Lewis said, pointing into the woods.

A middle-aged man with short brown hair, dressed in a tank top, long pants, and hiking boots appeared from around a bend in the trail. He walked fast and approached our position quickly as he pushed a one-wheeled device that looked like a unicycle without a seat.

"You must be my PATC reinforcements. Glad to have you," Myron Avery said to us.

"Glad to help, sir. What would you like us to do?" I asked.

Before Mr. Avery could respond, Hug-a-Bug asked, "Did your unicycle break?"

Mr. Avery laughed and responded, "It may look like a unicycle, but actually, this is a survey wheel. You hold this handle and push it along to measures distance. Here, let me show you how to use it, and you can measure the next section of trail with me."

"Awesome! I would be glad to help," Hug-a-Bug replied.

And so it went. We spent the next hour helping Mr. Avery's trail crew cut trees, move rocks, and mark the trail. Hug-a-Bug learned how to use a survey wheel and rolled it along to measure the trail, then she joined the rest of us to help move a tree that we had cut down off the trail. This was hard work. I had blisters on the palms of my hands from using the shovel, pick axe, and saw. Papa Lewis suggested we take a break, which was my cue to take us back to the present. We gathered together out of view of Myron Avery and the PATC crew and I said, "Take us back to the present."

Seconds later, a warm gust of wind blasted us and we were back in the parking lot next to our Jeep, parked along Skyline Drive.

"Wow, building the A.T. was hard work. We helped build a measly twenty-yard section. I can't imagine doing that work for 2,000-miles. We definitely earned our dinner," I said.

"You got that right," Hug-a-Bug said.

We climbed into the Jeep, buckled our seatbelts, and pulled out onto Skyline Drive northbound towards Loft Mountain Campground, our Shenandoah home for the night. The two-lane road took us around gentle curves with thick forest and wildflowers on either side and every so often, we would pass by a paved pull-off, lined with knee-high stone walls, with spectacular views of the Shenandoah Valley and the mountains in the distance.

"Guess where the park service ended up building Skyline Drive?" Papa Lewis asked.

"That's easy, right here alongside the Appalachian Trail," I answered.

"Not quite. Skyline Drive was built right on top of the original Appalachian Trail," Papa Lewis answered.

"I'm confused. Right now we're driving on Skyline Drive and the Appalachian Trail runs alongside the road," I stated.

"The A.T. was moved over when the road was built," Papa Lewis replied.

"You mean we just did all that work with Mr. Avery and the PATC crew for nothing?!" Hug-a-Bug asked exasperatedly. "Those poor hard-working trail crew members must have been quite upset when they learned their work was going to be covered by a road."

"I'm sure there were some upset PATC workers, but they literally had an ARMY to help them move the trail— more on that later! The man I mentioned earlier who inspired the A.T., Benton MacKaye, was very upset when he learned that the trail was going to parallel a road. Roads weren't part of his vision of a wilderness path. He was so upset that he removed himself from any involvement with the A.T. Meanwhile, Avery was determined to follow through and make sure the A.T. was built. Avery accepted the idea of Skyline Drive. This difference of opinion about the road caused a deep division between Avery and MacKaye. But Avery continued to build the A.T. and organized volunteers to help. Today, Skyline Drive remains the single greatest feature of Shenandoah National Park, and the A.T. is considered one of the world's most famous footpaths," Papa Lewis explained.

When we drove along Skyline Drive earlier, it had felt instead as if we were driving along the Appalachian Trail. Now it made sense, because we actually were driving along parts of the original footpath. Whitetail deer were everywhere. We had to stop suddenly when a young fawn speckled with white spots, still learning to run, clumsily stumbled into the road in pursuit of its mom.

"Hey Clark, pull into the next overlook," Papa Lewis requested.

Minutes later, Dad pulled off of Skyline Drive following a sign that read "Crimora Lake Overlook, elevation 2,975 ft." We all stepped out of the vehicle to enjoy the view. We could see far down into the valley, dotted with farmhouses, barns, patches of forest, and farm fields all the way across to distant mountains. I spotted Crimora Lake, a small body of water sandwiched between some mountains below us. A large black bird circled above us. I felt like a hawk, perched above the Shenandoah Valley and able to see far off into the distance.

"I stopped here with Cousin Nick many moons ago while we were exploring Shenandoah," Papa Lewis said with a bright gleam in his eyes.

"It sure is beautiful," commented Hug-a-Bug.

"It definitely is, Hug-a-Bug. The park name 'Shenandoah' is a Native American word that means 'beautiful daughter of the stars.'"

"That's a perfect name for the park," Hug-a-Bug commented.

"Your mom and grandma are expecting us back at camp for supper. We should probably head there now," Dad said as he hopped back in the Jeep.

"We'll continue to explore tomorrow. Right now, dinner sounds good," Papa Lewis replied as the rest of us hopped in the Jeep, pulled out onto Skyline Drive and headed towards Loft Mountain Campground.

A NIGHT ON THE MOUNTAIN

Ashort while later, a brown National Park Service sign alerted us that we had arrived at Loft Mountain Campground. It was late in the day and the sun was slowly sinking behind a distant mountain. Dad pulled off of Skyline Drive and into the campground. We passed another sign that read "Bear Country. Protect your property and food. Proper food storage is required."

Hug-a-Bug's eyes were glued to the bear warning sign as we drove by. "You mean we are going to sleep outside with bears that can destroy our property and take our food?" Hug-a-Bug asked.

"Don't you worry, Hug-a-Bug. You already have experience camping and hiking in areas with bears. The sign is meant to remind you that you're in bear country. We will store all our food and scented items, like deodorant, toothpaste, and soap, in the vehicle and away from our tent. You will be just fine," Papa Lewis replied.

It's always nice to get some reassurance from Papa Lewis, and Hug-a-Bug seemed to feel more at ease. I did, too.

"After we dropped you guys on the Appalachian Trail back at Rockfish Gap, the park ranger at the entrance station went over all the bear issues with us. Shenandoah has a large black bear population," Dad added.

Dad weaved the Jeep through the campground which was bustling with RVs, tents, and people of all ages. Smoke puffed up from fire rings while people sat at picnic tables eating and enjoying the mountaintop views.

"Shenandoah National Park has four campgrounds, and this is the largest of them," Papa Lewis explained.

Dad pulled into our campsite. I could see Mom and Grandma seated at the picnic table under our dining canopy, and it looked like they had dinner all ready to go. The table had an array of food placed assembly-line style at one end. I got excited as I noticed the ingredients: a jar of pizza sauce, a bag of shredded mozzarella cheese, chopped vegetables, pepperoni, a loaf of bread, and campfire pie irons. A small stream of smoke emanated from red-hot coals in the fire pit. My stomach growled. We were about to have one of my favorite camping meals.

"Pie iron pizzas for dinner! Awesome! Thank you, Mom and Grandma," I said, and Hug-a-Bug grinned and licked her lips in anticipation.

"We thought you guys would like this after your hike," Mom said.

We filled in Mom and Grandma on all the details of our hiking adventure, while Dad and Papa Lewis assembled slices of bread into the pie irons, filled them with pizza sauce, then added cheese and our favorite toppings. They clipped the pie irons shut and placed them carefully over the fire. Within minutes, we had hot pizza for everyone. We all sat down at the picnic table while mom poured lemonade into cups and passed them around the table until everybody had a drink.

"A nice view, great weather, family, and pie iron pizza. What more could you ask for?" I exclaimed as I devoured my meal.

"Well, we still haven't met up with the 'unknown relative' that led us here," Hug-a-Bug said.

We all had a deep suspicion that Papa Lewis' cousin Nick was behind the decoding tip that led us to Shenandoah. Nick and his family lived nearby in Charlottesville, Virginia. Papa had shared lots fond memories of his Shenandoah adventures with us. Many of them were with his cousin Nick. Like most of our family members, Nick is a time traveler. Each branch of our family specializes in a specific geographical region or park and uses their own trade or skill to preserve and protect our wildlands for future generations. Papa Lewis explained that Nick's branch has always been involved in protecting our family secret, and this includes secret codes. Apparently, ancestors from Nick's branch were spies that helped America win its freedom during the American Revolution. I only met Nick, his wife Dolly, and their son Washington once at a wedding years ago. I was just five, Hug-a-Bug was two, and Washington was four. This was long before I knew about our family time-travel skills. Nick and Dolly, who are similar in age to Papa Lewis and Grandma, had always wanted to be parents, but weren't able to have a child of their own. So, later in life they decided to adopt. They adopted a son,

John, and nicknamed him Washington in honor of our first president.

When Cousin Nick isn't exploring or protecting our family time-travel secret, he works for a top-secret government agency. We're not supposed to know about it, but since we've all been sworn to secrecy about our own time-travel ability, Cousin Nick knows that we'll never tell anyone. Besides, we don't really even know about what he does; only that it's a matter of national security.

Papa Lewis and Grandma contacted Cousin Nick and Dolly hoping to arrange to meet-up with them in Shenandoah. But they acted quite strange. They weren't their usual selves and were very indefinite about meeting up with us. Papa Lewis had a feeling it had something to do with Nick's work. Hug-a-Bug and I hoped that we would get a chance to spend time with Washington while we were in Shenandoah.

After dinner, we sat around the campfire and watched the logs burn down to smoldering red embers. Papa Lewis and Grandma were the first to go to bed. Shortly after, we secured all of our food and scented items in our vehicle and the rest of us zipped into the tent for the night.

We were all unsure of our plans for the next day, wondering if we would hear from Cousin Nick, and we were completely exhausted from the drive and hike. A cool breeze blew over the mountain and through the screen of the tent, which made for perfect sleeping conditions. I dozed right off and didn't wake up until the smell of bacon and coffee wafted through the air the next morning. I sat up in my sleeping bag. It was early in the morning, and the tent door was unzipped. I could see Papa Lewis sitting at the picnic table beneath the dining canopy sipping his morning coffee, and Grandma was standing in front of the camp stove perched on the edge of the picnic table, turning bacon over in the skillet. I slipped out of the tent and joined them while Hug-a-Bug, Dad, and Mom slept.

Several small whitetail deer grazed just yards from our picnic table, apparently unafraid of us. Morning birds chirped. Other folks around us began emerging from their tents and campers and began to prepare breakfast. Billows of smoke and the faint whistle of propane stoves began to drift through the campground. Moments later, Hug-a-Bug, Mom, and Dad joined us at the picnic table. Grandma heaped the plates with scrambled eggs and bacon, and passed them around to us.

"Thanks for making breakfast, Grandma," I said.

"Yes, thank you, Grandma," Hug-a-Bug chimed in.

Dad grabbed some orange juice from the cooler and we all sat down to eat. There was something special about eating a meal outside in the open air with family, on top of a mountain, with deer grazing nearby, that made it feel like a little bit of heaven.

Little did we know that our tranquil mountain morning was about to change. Papa Lewis had three park maps stacked in front of him, and when everyone finished breakfast, he unfolded one of them and began studying it. We all gathered around. Since we hadn't heard from Cousin Nick, Papa Lewis was planning to take us exploring to some of his favorite spots in the park.

"Shenandoah National Park is long and narrow, spanning miles. Skyline Drive is 105 miles long but the park is about 70 miles long (roughly Front Royal–Waynesboro) 'as the crow flies.' The park is split into three sections: the South district, the Central district, and the North district. Right now, we are in the South District and there is a lot to explore. I left Nick a message and let him know where we are at in the park. I haven't heard back from him. But, as I mentioned before, whoever is behind the coded message that led us here will contact us.

"Do you think your cousin Nick is the person who sent us the code tip?" I asked.

"He is capable of it, and this park is his area of expertise. Nick will keep you on your toes. He is always up to something. Nick adds an element to the adventure like no other," Papa Lewis explained.

Before Papa Lewis could respond, our conversation was interrupted by the sound of an approaching electric motor. A golf cart zipped along the campground drive, pulled into our campsite, and stopped. A man and woman wearing tan National Park Service volunteer uniforms emerged from the golf cart and approached us at the picnic table.

"Good morning! We're the campground hosts and we are looking for the Lewis and Clark clan," the man stated.

"Well, good morning! That's us," Papa Lewis stated.

"We have something for you," the woman stated holding up a sealed envelope.

I walked over and retrieved the envelope from her.

"Who gave this to you?" Dad asked.

"We don't know. Someone slipped it under the door of the ranger check-in station with the note 'Please deliver to the campsite of Lewis and Clark.' Your campsite is the only one registered under that name, so it was pretty easy to find you. Everyone up in the ranger station got a kick out of your camp registration name, by the way. The original Lewis and Clark duo were some true explorers," the woman responded.

"Thank you!" Dad said, grinning.

The campground hosts hopped back on their golf cart and motored on down the road.

I quickly tore open the envelope and pulled out a typed letter.

Everyone gathered around me to read the note:

Dear Family,

Sorry for the delay in greeting you here in Shenandoah. You're now in my backyard, and I would love to show you around. Well, it's not really my yard, but I grew up here and Shenandoah is where I explore. I heard that some of you hiked into the park along the Appalachian Trail yesterday. The Appalachian Trail is only a part of exploring Shenandoah, and you're about to discover what I mean. I switched our code system. Taped up under the front bumper of your vehicle is your new cipher code. Sorry for the secrecy. This is not only to protect our family time-travel secret; it has now also become a matter of national security. Here is your first destination:

ALVIBP   OFSBO   CXIIP

See you soon!

I got down on my hands and knees and ran my hand along the bottom surface of the front bumper until my fingers touched what felt like paper. I peered under the bumper and sure enough, there was a folded piece of paper taped there. I pulled it free, unfolded it, and discovered our new cipher code:

Plain	A	B	C	D	E	F	G	H	I	J	K	L	M
Cipher	X	Y	Z	A	B	C	D	E	F	G	H	I	J

Plain	N	O	P	Q	R	S	T	U	V	W	X	Y	Z
Cipher	K	L	M	N	O	P	Q	R	S	T	U	V	W

"Is this for real? A matter of national security? Really?" Hug-a-Bug asked.

"We have to assume so, Hug-a-Bug," Papa Lewis replied.

"Is this from your cousin Nick, or his son Washington? And how did he know we hiked on the A.T. yesterday?" I asked.

"It could be either Nick or Washington. I'm sure Nick has taught Washington everything he knows. Let's figure this code out. I believe this is a Caesar Cipher. It's one of the simplest and most common coding systems. To figure out each letter of the code, we need to match the cipher letters with plain text letters using our decoder sheet. We simply use the cipher code to convert each cipher letter in the message to the plain text letter above it and this will allow us to decode the message," Papa Lewis explained.

I followed Papa Lewis' advice and deciphered each word. This is what I got:

Plain: DOYLES   RIVER   FALLS

Cipher: ALVIBP   OFSBO   CXIIP

"Where is Doyles River Falls?" I asked Papa Lewis.

"We are just a few minutes from the Doyles River Falls Trail. I hiked that trail years ago with Cousin Nick. We can take the A.T. from our campsite to the trailhead. Think of Shenandoah as a tree; the Appalachian Trail and Skyline Drive are the trunk, and the 400 or so miles of other trails are the branches. The Appalachian Trail only covers 101 miles of over 500 miles of trail right here in the park. The A.T. thru-hikers who walk the trail in one season have too much ground to cover and usually miss most of these other Shenandoah gems. It looks like we are on a new quest. Are you guys up for the challenge?" Papa Lewis asked looking at all of us.

"I'm in," I said.

"Me, too," Hug-a-Bug replied.

"Of course," Dad stated.

"Sounds interesting," Mom answered.

"Let's get going," Grandma said with a smile.

Papa Lewis gave Grandma a hug. She has had difficulty with her hip and knees for some time and has not been able to hike with us. Her willingness to come along let us know that she must be feeling better.

CHAPTER 6

A Civil War Rendezvous

I n minutes, we had our daypacks outfitted with water, food, and gear. We grabbed our trekking poles and everybody slipped their packs on. The A.T. looped around Loft Mountain Campground so we simply walked out of our campsite and onto the Appalachian Trail. When we reached the A.T., we headed south. In a short while, we came to a trail junction. It was marked by a cement post with aluminum bands wrapped around it. The aluminum bands on the post indicated we had reached the Doyles River Falls Trail.

"All trail junctions in Shenandoah are marked with these posts. Always check the posts to make sure you're going in the right direction," Papa Lewis instructed.

We turned left onto the Doyles River Falls Trail and continued on. The trail descended rapidly. It was a hot summer day, but it was still cool under the canopy of the trees. After a while, the trail widened and we could hear the gurgling of a mountain stream. Tulip poplar trees towered over us as we descended farther down the mountain.

We crossed a wide gravel road which our map indicated was Browns Gap Road, a horse trail. We continued on.

"Remind me to tell you about that road on the way back up the mountain," Papa Lewis said.

We passed a small waterfall and kept walking. A short while later, we came to another cement trail post that indicated the upper falls were nearby on the left. We stopped for a few minutes to take in the view of water rushing over a small cliff before merging with the lower falls. Then we walked on a little farther and reached the lower falls. Everyone took off their packs and sat down to enjoy the view. White water poured down over ancient rocks and pooled near where we sat before flowing on down the mountain.

"The A.T. hikers will miss all these amazing waterfalls in Shenandoah unless they leave the A.T. and hike one of the park's side trails. There are many more of these stunning waterfalls in the park," Papa Lewis stated as we sat there enjoying the view and the sound of the waterfall.

"This is amazing! Now I see what you mean about missing the gems of Shenandoah if you don't veer off the A.T.," Hug-a-Bug said.

"Now would be a good time to eat a snack before we hike back up the mountain," Dad said.

Everyone unzipped their packs and dug out something to eat. I pulled an energy bar from my pack, tore open the wrapper, and wolfed it down while also guzzling water.

"Papa Lewis, I don't get it. We came all the way to Shenandoah National Park at the request of an unknown family member who we think is either Cousin Nick or Washington. We travel here and get a secret message that leads us to this waterfall. This is extremely beautiful and I'm glad I had the opportunity to enjoy this…but what does this have to do with national security? Why are we here?" I asked.

"Bubba Jones, you've asked the question I think we all want to know the answer to. I know Cousin Nick, and he does things for a reason. I'm sure we will find out soon enough."

After we all finished our snacks, we stood up, put our packs back on, and retraced our steps back up the mountain. We let Grandma set the pace. She moved slowly, but it was good to have her along on the trail. The climb back up was strenuous compared to the hike down to the water fall. We reached Browns Gap Road and stopped. There was fresh horse manure on the road, indicating recent use. Moments later, Papa Lewis caught up to us and stopped. He wiped the sweat from his forehead with a handkerchief tied to the shoulder strap of his pack.

"Well, Papa Lewis, you said to remind you to tell us about this road," I said.

"This is a horse path now, but at one point in history this path was a toll road, and you had to pay to pass over the mountain. This mountain pass, along with a few other mountain gaps in Shenandoah, played a strategic role for Thomas 'Stonewall' Jackson during the Civil War."

"Who was Thomas 'Stonewall' Jackson?" Hug-a-Bug asked.

"Jackson was one of the most successful Civil War generals. He was known as the 'lightning bolt of the Confederacy.' He was completely outnumbered by the

Union Army, but he used the Blue Ridge Mountains to confuse, outmaneuver, and defeat the opposing army."

"Wait a minute. Did you say 'Confederacy?' The Confederates lost the war. How can he be one of the most successful generals?" Hug-a-Bug asked.

"The Confederate Army relied on the Shenandoah Valley for food and supplies. Jackson only had an army of roughly 17,000 men. But he was able to move much faster than the larger Union Army of over 45,000 soldiers. He used the present day Shenandoah National Park, then simply known as the Blue Ridge Mountains, to hide his troop movements and confuse the enemy. Even today, his war strategy is studied worldwide because of the success of his tactics."

"How can you look up to the general of an army that fought to keep slavery?" I asked Papa Lewis.

"The Civil War was a sad time for our country. The fact that we had slavery here in the free world is horrible. Today it is hard to believe that slavery even existed. Over 600,000 soldiers died during the Civil War. That's almost more deaths then all other U.S. wars combined. I'm so glad that the Union won the war. Otherwise, this great country might still be divided, and slavery, sadly, might have continued. Just prior to the Civil War, President Abraham Lincoln was elected, and he was opposed to slavery. The southern states profited big-time from slave labor and did not want Lincoln interfering with this industry. Slaves worked on sprawling southern plantations which were owned by wealthy people. When Lincoln took office, eleven southern states seceded from the Union and formed the Confederacy. Virginia was one of those states. If you lived in one of the southern states, your loyalty was split. The country was divided. Families were torn apart by the question, 'Do you support your state or do you support the Union?' It wasn't long before war broke out. Able-bodied men were required by the laws of their state to enlist. Brothers, cousins, fathers, and sons fought alongside and against each other. Most of the soldiers who fought for the Confederacy didn't own slaves. Many families on both sides lost fathers and sons on the battlefield.

"Jackson, like other officers in the Confederacy, was originally an officer in the United States Army. 'Stonewall' was a nickname he earned from his battlefield tactics. The way Stonewall led his army to victory on the battlefield is the reason he is viewed as successful, regardless of whether his side ultimately won the war. He was shot by his own men by accident in 1863, and the Confederacy didn't do very well after that. Some historians believe his death was the reason the South lost the war, and almost all historians believe that Jackson was one of the most successful generals the Confederates had," Papa Lewis explained.

"What do you say we go back and see what it was like in Shenandoah when Jackson's army came through?" I suggested.

"I figured you would want to do that. Only a few small battles occurred in what is now Shenandoah National Park. Most of the fighting that took place in this region happened down in the Shenandoah Valley and elsewhere. Let's go back to early June 1862. That is one of the times Jackson crossed his army over the Blue Ridge on Browns

Gap Toll Road and rested up before he led them to battle near Richmond, Virginia," Papa Lewis explained.

We all gathered around in a circle on Browns Gap Road. I said, "Take us back to June 10th, 1862."

A gust of wind blew. Everything went dark and then our surroundings completely changed. Large sections of the forest we had stood in moments ago were now cleared pastures with horses grazing in them. Rows of canvas tents lined the road and continued up a grass-covered hillside to the lawn of a log home, then continued on as far as the eye could see. Long wooden rifles were stacked in circular bunches in front of the tents. Men in grey uniforms were everywhere. Smoke billowed up from fire pits, emitting the smell of roasting meat, and metal coffee pots sat on iron grates over fires, steam swirling from their spouts.

Our clothes had transformed. I wore a straw hat with a wide brim, long wool pants, a cotton shirt, and boots. Papa Lewis and Dad wore much the same, except they both had on black top hats. Hug-a-Bug, Grandma, and Mom all wore colorful long sleeve, full length dresses with full, billowing skirts, and they had bonnets on their heads.

We stood in the middle of Browns Gap Road, taking everything in. I noticed a man and woman similar in age to Papa Lewis and Grandma standing with a boy about my age next to a horse-drawn wagon parked along the side of the road. The horse's reins were wrapped around a fence post. The wagon was loaded with bags of corn-meal, baskets of berries, potatoes, and onions, and crates containing live chickens. The family appeared to be local farmers, but they looked strangely familiar.

The pounding of hooves suddenly shook the ground. I turned to look, and saw two endless columns of grey-uniformed soldiers on horseback thundering towards us. It's not often you see Civil War soldiers from over 150 years ago approaching, and we stood transfixed.

"Get out of the road!" a voice hollered, and a hand clamped onto my shoulder and yanked me backwards. We all just made it off of Browns Gap Road seconds before the stream of soldiers and horses rushed by, leaving a cloud of dust in their wake. Picking myself up from the ground, I looked back to see who pulled me to safety. It was the same farm boy I had noticed before.

"Thanks for saving me!" I exhaled, still trying to catch my breath.

"Bubba Jones, they don't have traffic lights and crosswalks yet! You need to give way to riders, especially soldiers! That was Stonewall Jackson and his officers that just rode by!" the farm boy exclaimed.

He knows my name…that's why he and his folks look familiar. It's Cousin Nick, Dolly, and Washington! I thought.

"Washington, is that you?" I asked the boy.

"Yes. Don't make a scene. Act like you're with us," Washington whispered.

"Wow! Just when I think I've seen it all, I meet up with you guys in the middle of our time travel. This is awesome!" I said.

CHAPTER 7

THE CIPHER MASTER REVEALED

ousin Nick lowered his voice so he wouldn't be over-heard by the soldiers. "We've been expecting you guys. It's good to see you. But we have to act like we're together and we're supposed to be here, so no hugs or greetings. Walk with us over to our wagon. If anyone asks where you're from, just say you're staying with us in Charlottesville. Don't mention anything about living in Ohio."

We followed Cousin Nick, Dolly, and Washington back over to the wagon.

"What's wrong with living in Ohio?" Hug-a-Bug asked.

"Ohio was part of the Union during the Civil War and you're in the middle of a Confederate Army camp. They'll think we're spies," Cousin Nick whispered.

"Yikes! What will they do if they think we're spies? By the way, you guys are the ones acting like spies, sending us secret codes," Hug-a-Bug replied.

"Keep it down! And you don't want to find out what they do to spies. We figured meeting you back in time was the safest place, due to our national security assignment.

We thought that if you went down the Doyles River Falls Trail, your Papa Lewis would remember our Brown Gap Road time-travel adventure years ago and you would time travel back to Stonewall's camp, like Lewis and I did. Dolly, Washington, and I time traveled back just before you and it looks like our plan worked."

Just then, two mounted soldiers split away from the group that had galloped past us moments ago and trotted over in our direction. I thought for sure they were suspicious of us.

"Let me do the talking and go along with whatever I say," Cousin Nick hissed.

The men pulled up their horses next to the wagon.

"I reckon you're looking to sell us some supplies," a bearded soldier said, remaining on his horse as he examined the contents of the wagon.

"That's right. We figured ya'll could use some extra food," Cousin Nick replied.

The other soldier dismounted and tied his horse to a nearby hitching post. He removed his leather riding gloves, opened one of his saddle bags, and pulled out a leather pouch stuffed with cash. Walking over to the wagon, he took inventory of all the supplies.

"Here's $5.00 for everything. I hope that's enough. I'll have my men unload your wagon."

"That will be just fine," Cousin Nick replied.

We all stood by silently as the soldier walked over to a nearby row of tents and ordered some men to unload the wagon. I was nervous the whole time, thinking about what could happen if they suspected we were spies. Fortunately, they never asked us where we were from.

After the wagon was unloaded, we all climbed up into the empty wagon bed. Cousin Nick and Papa Lewis climbed up into the buckboard seat and Cousin Nick took up the reigns and guided the wagon down Browns Gap Road.

We drove away, out of view of the camp. A few hundred yards down the road, we were stopped by soldiers at a perimeter checkpoint. They held rifles tipped with bayonets at the ready. Since we were leaving the Confederate camp rather than entering, we didn't pose a threat, so they let us pass without asking any questions. Cousin Nick drove the wagon a good half mile down the road and then pulled up the horse. We were now way out of sight of the armed soldiers.

"That was scary. The whole time I was imagining what would happen if they suspected that we were spies," I said.

"Imagine if the Union had known where Jackson's army was camped. It could have changed the outcome of the battle or even the war. Imagine if scientists knew precisely when and how the fungus from Asia that wiped out the American chestnut trees would arrive in the U.S. They could have stopped it from killing millions of trees. These seem like some positive ways our time-travel ability could be used. But imagine if it was used by someone to find all the gold mines in the country. Imagine if it was used by someone to go back and give the Confederates better guns or more men to help them win. Imagine if you stopped the Asian fungus that killed the American chestnuts and then found out you actually cleared the way for another far more destructive fungus that took its place and wiped out even more species of trees. We should only use our time travel to learn about the past. We must never use it to change history," Cousin Nick explained.

We fell silent, thinking about Cousin Nick's words. I broke the silence with a question that had been on my mind.

"So, who is writing the coded messages, and why is our secret a matter of national security?" I asked.

Cousin Nick looked over at Washington. There was a long pause. Then Washington looked over at all of us.

"I'm the one writing the messages. Our time-travel secret is not a matter of national security, but something I'm working on here in the park is, and I'm not allowed to say what it is right now. Until my assignment is over, we can only meet in secret. Back in time is the safest way," Washington said.

"How could you be working on a national security secret? You're only a kid. And where did you learn how to write cipher codes?" I asked.

In the conversation that followed, Cousin Nick, Dolly, and Washington caught us up on what had been going on since we had last seen them, some time ago. When Washington was five years old, Cousin Nick held a work meeting in his home with some top secret colleagues. No one in the agency ever thought to worry about Washington overhearing them; he was only five, after all. Cousin Nick and Dolly were already a bit startled by Washington's advanced reading level; he learned to read chapter books at the age of four, but that was nothing compared to what came next. While Cousin Nick was going over confidential information with his work colleagues, he had laid out encoded documents on the coffee table in the living room. Since the contents were written in cipher, no one in the meeting worried about Washington seeing them as he played with his little toy cars on the floor near the coffee table. No one became alarmed when Washington left the room and returned with a pen and paper, kneeled down at the coffee table, and began writing things down. Cousin Nick and his colleagues were right there next to the coffee table and Washington was in full sight. According to a debriefing on their security breach after the incident, everyone assumed that a five-year-old with a pen and paper would either be drawing stick figures or attempting to write some basic kindergarten-level words. They continued on with their meeting. Meanwhile, Washington finished writing and then he left his note and pen on the coffee table next to the documents and went back to playing with his cars, zooming them around on the floor.

It wasn't until the end of the meeting when one of Nick's colleagues went to pick up the documents that it was discovered what Washington had done: he had decoded the secret messages embedded in the documents. This caused major panic within the top secret agency. It baffled everyone. How could a little kid decode their top secret messages? Cousin Nick was interrogated for days to make sure he wasn't behind this. This made him nervous, because none of his colleagues knew about our family time-travel secret and this incident drew attention to his family. He was afraid they would question Washington, and Washington might reveal the secret. After the panic at the agency died down, they not only changed the way they handle encoded documents, they also realized that Washington's talent with code breaking could help the agency. And that is how Washington became their youngest employee.

Cousin Nick and Dolly had Washington evaluated by several child experts. It was concluded that while Washington appeared to be an ordinary, typical five-year-old, he had extraordinary intelligence. He maxed out every IQ test with a perfect score. Cousin Washington was off -the- charts genius, well beyond some adults with PhDs. He could see patterns that most people could not. He could quickly think through difficult equations that he had never learned.

Nick and Dolly wanted Washington to grow up and experience all the things a normal kid does as much as possible, in spite of his extraordinary abilities. An arrangement was made with the agency so that Washington's skills would only be used if it was a matter of national security. Washington attended school and played sports like the other kids his age. But, unlike most other kids, he was occasionally called in by the agency to decipher a code for them. He also learned about our family time-traveling ability and inherited the ability from his father, just as I had from Papa Lewis. Cousin Nick and Dolly took Washington into Shenandoah National Park nearly every week. Together, they explored every inch of the park, carrying out our family's mission to protect and preserve our wildlands for future generations. Then, just days before our arrival to Shenandoah, Cousin Nick was notified that they needed to activate Washington. It was a matter of national security, and it had to do with

Shenandoah National Park. It explained why Cousin Nick acted strangely with Papa Lewis when he tried to make arrangements to meet up with them.

Washington handed me a folded piece of paper similar to the note that was under our Jeep this morning.

"Here's your next Shenandoah adventure. Put this in your pocket and it will be with you when you travel back to the present."

"So you're not going to go back with us? Bubba Jones and I were really looking forward to hanging out with you." Hug-a-Bug said.

"I can't until this project is finished. But we will meet up with you during our time-travel adventures. We can explore the park together that way. It will be fun."

"How did you know we hiked on the A.T. yesterday?" I asked.

"We're members of the PATC and friends with the trail crew that you met yesterday," Washington answered.

"We should probably head back to the future now. We must travel back separately from you. We were riding on horseback along Browns Gap Road when we time traveled to Jackson's camp, so we'll remain with the horse and wagon. You will have to wait until we are a good distance away before you time travel back to the present," Cousin Nick explained.

We said goodbye, gave hugs, and then Papa Lewis, Dad, Mom, Grandma, Hug-a-Bug, and I hopped down from the wagon. Cousin Nick grabbed the reins, shook them and said "Yaa," and the horse trotted off down the road. We turned to go when suddenly there was a loud kaboom. Turning back, we saw the horse and wagon standing by the side of the road. No one was in the wagon – they had already left. We all huddled together, and I said, "Take us back to the present."

CHAPTER 8

IF THESE ROCKS COULD TALK

A warm gust of air struck us as we traveled back to the present. We all stood on Browns Gap Road in our modern clothing. Sweat still dripped down my forehead from our hike up from the waterfall, as if we had never left. This seemed unreal. Did we really just meet our Virginia family at a Civil War camp?! I reached into my pocket and felt a folded up piece of paper. I pulled it out and sure enough, it was the note Washington gave to me moments ago in Civil War time.

Everyone was eager to know what the note said, but our stomachs came first. Walking down and up a mountain and then time traveling to the Civil War sure did work up an appetite! When we arrived back at our camp, we broke out the cooler from the Jeep and assembled some deli sandwiches, carrots, chips, and lemonade for lunch. When everyone was done eating, I unfolded the note and placed it on the picnic table to see what Washington had in store for us.

Bubba Jones and Family, Use the same code that led you to Jackson's camp to decipher this message. See you soon.

ZXISXOV   OLZHP   QEBK   YIXZHOLZH

I unfolded the cipher and plain text decoder sheet from earlier and went through each group of letters.

Plain	A	B	C	D	E	F	G	H	I	J	K	L	M
Cipher	X	Y	Z	A	B	C	D	E	F	G	H	I	J

Plain	N	O	P	Q	R	S	T	U	V	W	X	Y	Z
Cipher	K	L	M	N	O	P	Q	R	S	T	U	V	W

This was the message I deciphered.

Plain: CALVARY   ROCKS   THEN   BLACKROCK

Cipher: ZXISXOV   OLZHP   QEBK   YIXZHOLZH

"Well, I know right where those are located. They are both in the South District. Both are short hikes with easy access from Skyline Drive. It will be best to drive to each trailhead and walk from there. Who's in?" Papa Lewis asked.

Grandma, Mom, and Dad decided to stay back at camp together. Grandma was tuckered out after our waterfall hike, and Mom and Dad needed time to prepare our evening meal. Papa Lewis handed me the map. "I'll drive, you navigate," Papa Lewis said.

Hug-a-Bug, Papa Lewis, and I replenished the snacks and water in our packs, hopped in the Jeep, and drove out of the campground.

"We're going to the Riprap parking area. We have to drive back towards the Rockfish Gap entrance where we entered the park to milepost ninety, along Skyline Drive. That's the closest trailhead to Calvary Rocks. Each mile along Skyline Drive is marked by a cement post etched with the mileage in black. We have about ten miles to go," Papa Lewis explained.

In minutes we had arrived at the Riprap parking area. We hoisted our packs onto our backs, grabbed our trekking poles, and away we went down the trail, Papa Lewis bringing up the rear. The walk was easy, and in no time we reached Calvary Rocks. Large gray boulders jutted up from the earth with countless vertical lines etched into them.

"Those are weird-looking rocks," Hug-a-Bug commented.

"Those lines are trace fossils called Skolithos linearis. They were sand tubes left by worms that lived in beach sand in the ancient Iapetus Ocean, which predated the Atlantic Ocean," Papa Lewis explained.

"Are you thinking what I'm thinking?" I asked, looking at Hug-a-Bug.

"Uh-huh! Let's go to the beach, Bubba Jones," Hug-a-Bug said.

"It is estimated that the Iapetus Ocean existed 400 to 600 million years ago. To be safe, let's go back to July 15th 500 million years ago," Papa Lewis explained.

I clutched the family journal and said, "Take us back to July 15th 500 million years ago."

A gust of hot air knocked us back. Everything went dark. Then I felt sand between my toes. I looked down and saw I was standing in shallow water. Our clothes had been replaced with bathing suits. A warm breeze ruffled my hair, and a gentle wave splashed against us.

"Hey guys, come on over and join us on the beach," a familiar voice shouted.

We turned and looked over our shoulders. There sat Washington, Cousin Nick, and Dolly on a sandy beach, basking in the sun. The three of us waded out of the water and onto the beach. Our valley view was now endless ocean.

"Lewis, I'm glad you remembered the time we visited this ancient beach. We've been taking Washington here since he was a toddler," Cousin Nick said.

"Where are the worms that left those vertical fossils in Calvary Rock?" Hug-a-Bug asked.

"Those rocks were once beach sand. So the worms are buried underneath in the water," Papa Lewis explained.

Papa Lewis, Cousin Nick, and Dolly sat in the sand and talked while Washington, Hug-a-Bug, and I ran down the beach and jumped into the ancient ocean. We swam and took turns burying each other in the sand as if we were at Virginia Beach on the Atlantic Ocean. We completely lost ourselves in the fun.

"See, I told you we would have fun. It's a time-traveling vacation!" Washington said.

"This is unbelievable! We're playing on a 500 million-year-old beach that no longer exists. Shouldn't we be worried about dinosaurs?" Hug-a-Bug asked.

"No dinosaurs yet. Those came a few hundred million years later," Washington said.

"I'm getting confused about what happened when. All of our time-travel episodes have been out of order, and I'm not that good at history to start with. It's hard to keep track of *when* we are, much less what happened then. I mean when. I don't even know what I mean!" Hug-a-Bug said.

"You should make a timeline, Hug-a-Bug. You can keep track of where you've been and place the events in order from oldest to most recent," Washington suggested.

"That's a great idea!" Hug-a-Bug responded enthusiastically.

"We should probably get going to Blackrock," Washington said.

"Sounds like a plan," I added.

We all walked over to where Papa Lewis, Cousin Nick, and Dolly sat on the beach.

"Ready to move on?" Cousin Nick asked us.

"Let's go!" I stated.

"See you in few," Washington said as he walked away with Cousin Nick and Dolly.

"Yep, see you at Blackrock," I said.

Papa Lewis, Hug-a-Bug, and I stood and watched them walk away along the beach, and then a loud *kaboom* shook us, and they were gone. We all stood together and I said "Take us back to the present."

A gust of warm air swirled around us. Everything went dark and then lit back up and we found ourselves once again standing next to the ancient rocks with the worm holes. We had our modern clothes and packs on once again. On our walk back to the parking area, we passed a family walking towards Calvary Rocks.

"Enjoy the ancient beach," I said with a grin to the family as they passed us.

The mom and dad gave a confused smile. I heard one of their kids exclaim as they continued on, "Mom, Dad, you didn't tell us we're hiking to a beach!"

Hug-a-Bug looked over at me with a grin as we continued our hike back to our vehicle. This really brought home how amazing it was to be able to time travel back and experience history!

When we reached the parking lot, we threw our gear in the back of the Jeep, hopped into the vehicle, clicked on our seatbelts, and pulled onto Skyline Drive headed north, back towards Loft Mountain Campground. Papa Lewis never asked me for directions and a few minutes later he turned off of Skyline Drive and into another parking lot. He had definitely been here before. He brought the Jeep to a halt and shifted it into park.

"This walk is even shorter than Calvary Rocks—it's just a half-mile stroll. When we get to Blackrock, we will time travel back to the same period that Bubba Jones did when we encountered the woolly mammoth, at the end of the last ice age," Papa Lewis said.

We grabbed our gear and walked together down the trail towards Blackrock. It only took us a few minutes to reach our destination. The shaded trail opened up to a mountaintop covered with large broken pieces of gray rock. The rock chunks looked like a massive rubble pile after an earthquake. The rocks completely covered the mountaintop and ran down the mountain, deep into a forested hollow, out of view. This barren pile of rocks stood out against the surrounding lush, green, tree-covered mountains. It was really odd, as if this place had imploded among the others.

"What happened here?" I asked Papa Lewis.

"As the climate thawed then froze again at the end of the last ice age, it broke up large rocks into this rubble field that covers the entire mountaintop. It's called a talus slope. This happened during the periglacial period. There were no actual glaciers in Shenandoah, but it was still extremely cold. Towards the end of the ice age, the temperature would go back and forth between warm and cold," Papa Lewis explained. "Bubba Jones, take us back to July 16th 11,000 years ago."

I placed my hand on the family journal and said, "Take us back to July 16th, 11,000 years in the past."

A cold gust of air blew us backward. Everything went dark. We heard a snap, and then it became light again. We now stood at the top of a large stone cliff. Our clothes were replaced with deerskin and our feet were wrapped in animal hide. An icy wind gave me the chills, and goose bumps popped out on my arms. Washington, Cousin Nick, and Dolly were already there to greet us.

"Come over here and check out the view, guys," Washington hollered to us as they stood near the edge of the cliff looking outward.

We walked over to take a peek. The valley was completely covered in forest. No roads or farm fields dotted the land, just endless trees across the entire Shenandoah Valley. As we stood there, I thought it would be a good time to find out some more about what Washington was working on.

"Washington, why is your Shenandoah project so secret that you can't share it with us? I mean, we all have to hide that we can time travel, so it's not as if we don't know how to keep a secret!"

"Yeah, what could be so secret? Are you protecting something? Tracking something?" Hug-a-Bug asked as she crossed her arms, shivering from the cold.

We were interrupted by Cousin Nick, "Be careful everyone. The rock we're standing on could crumble and break off at any moment."

We all took a step back away from the cliff edge, realizing the danger we were in.

"Argh! This is frustrating, not being able to tell you guys what I'm doing! Yes, Hug-a-Bug, I'm monitoring something and it's related to our family mission of protecting and preserving this wildland. It may be a few days before we're able to meet up again. We have some work we need to do that will require us to stay up through the night. I will contact you as soon as we're done," Washington explained.

Just then, the ground beneath our feet shook. Large cracks appeared in the rock. It felt like the entire mountain was going to collapse beneath us.

"This doesn't look good. We better time travel out of here now!" Papa Lewis yelled over the thunder of rocks smashing and breaking up beneath our feet.

Just then, an entire slab of rock where Cousin Nick, Dolly, and Washington stood broke free from the mountain. For a split second, they seemed to stand in thin air, then, they plummeted downward. Cousin Nick held Washington's and Dolly's hands as they disappeared from view in a free fall.

"We'll catch up to you guys later," Cousin Nick yelled as they fell out of sight.

Papa Lewis, Hug-a-Bug, and I stood close together. The rocks beneath our feet began to separate as I screamed, "Take us back to the present!"

A warm gust of air blew us upward. Everything went dark. I blinked my eyes and we were once again standing on the trail, dressed in our modern clothes, our packs on our backs, in view of the rock field and the talus slopes.

"We have to go back and make sure they're okay," Hug-a-Bug panted.

"We can't. It's too dangerous. You heard Cousin Nick say they would catch up to us later," Papa Lewis replied.

"But they fell off a cliff! How can we be sure they were able to time travel back to the present?" I asked, "And Washington didn't give us a new cipher. Where do we go from here? What do we do?"

CHAPTER 9

A BLACKBERRY MOOD

Papa Lewis wrapped his arms around Hug-a-Bug and me and said, "Let's wait and see what happens. You don't know Cousin Nick like I do. I'm sure they are just fine."

Hug-a-Bug and I trudged back to the Jeep. We threw our packs and poles into the back, buckled in, and sat quietly as Papa Lewis pulled out onto Skyline Drive and headed north towards our campground.

"You both deserve a special Shenandoah treat. Have you ever had a blackberry milkshake?" Papa Lewis asked as he pulled into the Loft Mountain Wayside, a roadside restaurant and gift shop near our campground.

After hiking three different trails today, ice cream did sound good. We hopped out of the Jeep and walked with Papa Lewis up towards the Wayside entrance.

"Look, those are the thru-hikers' backpacks! The ones we hiked with a few days ago," Hug-a-Bug said, pointing to three backpacks lined up against the outside wall of the building along with three pairs of hiking poles, near the entrance.

We stepped inside and sure enough, the three hikers we met at Rockfish Gap stood looking at the menu posted over the counter. "Hey guys, we meet again," I said to the hikers.

"Hey, it's Bubba Jones and Hug-a-Bug! We didn't think we would see you again. Sorry about our pace. We didn't realize you had fallen behind until we ran into a PATC trail crew and stopped to talk with them. After that, we just wanted to get to the shelter for the night and eat dinner," one of the hikers explained.

"That's okay. We had a fun hike into the park after driving all day, and your pace was way too fast for us," I said.

"By the way, my trail name is Soul Search, that's Bagel Man, and that's Fungus," Soul Search said pointing to his buddies. "Thru-hikers take on nicknames as part of the trail culture."

"Have you all had the blackberry milkshake before? It's one of my favorite Shenandoah treats. They serve them at all the waysides. I'm buying. Would you like one?" Papa Lewis said invitingly.

Papa Lewis got a quick yes from the thru-hikers and placed an order for six blackberry milkshakes. We then we sat at a nearby table and slurped them down. Now I understood why Papa Lewis liked these shakes. They didn't take away our worry about our cousins, but they sure did hit the spot after a day of hiking.

The three thru-hikers planned to stay the night at Loft Mountain Campground, where we were camping. It's not often you get hot showers while hiking the Appalachian Trail, but three of the four campgrounds in Shenandoah had shower houses, and the A.T. skirted by each one. We offered to drive them into the campground, but they refused. Soul Search explained that they had walked off the A.T. to hit the Wayside, and they wanted to retrace their steps back to where they left the trail so they wouldn't skip any sections of the A.T. Like many thru-hikers, they wanted to make sure they hiked every inch of the A.T.

We said goodbye to the thru-hikers and parted with them in the parking lot. In a few minutes, we arrived back at our campground. Mom, Dad, and Grandma had dinner ready to throw on the fire whenever we were ready. We caught them up on our time-travel adventures to Calvary Rock and Black Rock. We explained what happened with Washington, Dolly, and Cousin Nick, and we told them about going to the Wayside and running into the thru-hikers we met at Rockfish Gap the other day, and how Papa Lewis treated us all to blackberry milkshakes.

"I love those blackberry milkshakes," Dad said with a smile.

Dad and Grandpa placed a steel grilling grate over the fire to cook Dad's special campfire steak, while Mom and Grandma sat in their camp chairs, reading books. Meanwhile, Hug-a-Bug sat down at the picnic table with pen and paper and began working on her timeline. She planned to organize all of our time-travel adventures in chronological order based on the time period we visited, from oldest to most recent.

It felt good to sit down after all our exploring. I stared at the fire, lost in thought. What was Washington working on out here that was so secret he couldn't share it with us? Were Cousin Nick, Dolly, and Washington safe after their fall during our Blackrock time-travel episode?

I replayed in my mind what Washington had said about his secret mission back at Blackrock. "I'm monitoring something and it's related to our family mission of protecting and preserving this wildland. It may be a few days before we're able to meet up again. We have some work we need to do that will require us to stay up all night. I will contact you as soon as I'm done."

Hug-a-Bug came over to show me her timeline and I shared some of my thoughts with her about Washington's secret mission.

"Cousin Crockett would be great to have along right now. If he knew about Washington's secret mission like us, he would want to figure out what all the secrecy was about," I said to Hug-a-Bug.

Cousin Crockett, and his parents, Uncle Boone and Aunt Walks-a-Lot, joined us in the Smokies on our last adventure. Cousin Crockett had really wanted to come along to Shenandoah, but his parents had business to tend to back home in Georgia, so we parted ways with them and came here.

"Cousin Crockett was a huge help with our family mystery. You're right; he would be good to have along right now," Hug-a-Bug replied.

Dad and Papa Lewis removed the fire-seared steaks, corn on the cob, sweet potatoes, and roasted green peppers from the grill, signaling that dinner was about to be served. Mom and Grandma placed a fresh salad and rolls on the table to go along with the grilled food. While we all sat around the picnic table devouring the delicious meal, we discussed our Shenandoah adventure.

"We were led here by Washington, Cousin Nick, and Dolly, but now they are on some secret mission that we are not supposed to know about. So, what do we do from here?" I asked.

Everyone looked at Papa Lewis for an answer.

"I spent many adventures in Shenandoah, and there is so much to see and do. Tomorrow we'll break camp and head north into the central district section of the park," Papa Lewis said as he unfolded the Central District map and spread it out on the picnic table for all of us to see.

We all circled around Papa Lewis to see what he had in store.

"I've made arrangements for us to stay a night here in the Pocosin Cabin," Papa Lewis explained pointing to a little cabin symbol near milepost sixty along Skyline Drive on the Appalachian Trail.

"That's cool. I didn't know there were cabins here," I said.

"Yep, the PATC maintains six cabins in Shenandoah National Park. We hiked past one today on our waterfall hike. All the cabins have bunks with mattresses, cookware, pit toilets, and a nearby spring. It will be easier to make camp there and explore the area instead of pitching the tent for just one night," Papa Lewis explained.

Hug-a-Bug and I didn't stay up very long after the sun went down. We were exhausted, and unlike most nights, we were the first ones to head to bed. I fell asleep as soon as my head hit the pillow. I slept straight through the night and woke up to the sound of the coffee pot gurgling.

Through the unzipped tent flap I could see Papa Lewis and Grandma seated at the picnic table. I slipped on my sandals and joined them.

"Good morning," I whispered.

"Good morning, Bubba Jones. Let's go pick some fruit to go along with breakfast," Papa Lewis whispered back.

We walked out onto the campground road, not talking so as not to wake other campers. Several deer grazed nearby. The morning dew clung to the blades of grass. Birds chirped, singing their morning song. We walked a few hundred feet down the road to a patch of grass with several apple trees loaded with low-hanging fruit. Papa Lewis started picking the apples, placing them in a sack he had brought along.

"Where did these apple trees come from? Are they native to Shenandoah National Park?"

"No, they are not native to this area. This campground sits on top of Big Flat Mountain. It used to be all pastures and fruit orchards. Cows used to graze here. It was owned by the Patterson family and maintained by the Frazier family. This apple tree is a remnant of one of their orchards. There are apple trees scattered throughout the park. Apples were grown by the mountain families that once called this area home. They would sell the apples for income. Now the bears, deer, birds, and us campers and hikers can enjoy them," Papa Lewis explained.

"I thought Shenandoah National Park was a wilderness area. I didn't realize people used to live here."

"Hardly an acre is original old-growth forest. What you see today is a second-growth forest. About 40 percent of the park is now also designated by Congress as wilderness and all the land is protected as a national park. But until this became a park in 1935, the land was privately owned. Much of the land had been cleared for grazing and crops. The timber was also heavily used as a resource by mountain residents and timber companies," Papa Lewis explained.

"You would never know it. Our entire Shenandoah experience so far has been in thick forest."

"It's amazing how fast the natural world, if allowed, can reestablish itself. You have to know what you're looking for to find signs of the human history. We'll explore more of this as we move along through the park. I think we have enough apples. We better get these back so your grandma can make her special fried apples for breakfast," Papa Lewis said.

We walked back to camp and helped Grandma peel and cut the apples. She put them in a skillet on our two-burner camp stove perched on the end of the picnic table. She added butter, sugar, and cinnamon, and then she lit the burner and let them simmer. Soon the sweet smell of apples and cinnamon drew the rest of the family members out of their tents. In no time, we had a huge breakfast of eggs, bacon, and fried apples. Hug-a-Bug and I put the fried apples on the top of our list of awesome yummy Grandma food!

After breakfast, we all helped break camp and pack up. After we loaded everything in the Jeep, Dad drove us out of Loft Mountain Campground and we continued north on Skyline Drive. We passed by the Swift Run Gap park entrance, which was another area where Confederate

General Jackson crossed through the mountains during the Civil War.

Everyone was enjoying the ride. Skyline Drive gently eased over the top of the mountain and around bends, opening up to spectacular views of the valley below, before slipping beneath the forest canopy.

Up ahead, we could see that cars were slowing down, and several had pulled off to the side of the road. Then traffic came to a sudden halt. Something must be wrong, I thought as we sat there in stopped traffic. People emerged from their vehicles and ran up ahead with their cameras at the ready.

"We might as well join them and see what all the fuss is about instead of just sitting here," Papa Lewis suggested.

Dad pulled our vehicle a safe distance off to the side of the road and Papa Lewis, Hug-a-Bug, and I jumped out of the Jeep, while Dad, Mom, and Grandma stayed back in the vehicle.

CHAPTER 10

FROM ONE MISSION TO ANOTHER

Papa Lewis stopped short of a large group of people that had gathered along the road and into the tree line. They were snapping pictures and pointing.

"Just what I suspected, a bear jam! All this traffic stopped to watch those bears. That's why they call it a bear jam instead of a traffic jam," Papa Lewis explained, pointing towards the tree line off to the right side of the road.

Hug-a-Bug and I looked over to where Papa Lewis was pointing, and sure enough, there were three black bear cubs high up in an oak tree hugging the trunk with their little legs. A large adult momma bear stood down on the ground at the base of the tree. She was protecting her cubs, standing between the mob of people snapping pictures and her cubs.

"It's never a good idea to come between a momma bear and her cubs, and you should never approach any bear. As a rule of thumb, you should keep at least fifty yards away," Papa Lewis advised.

The cubs slowly inched back down from the tree. We snapped some pictures from where we stood, a safe distance away. When the cubs reached the ground, the momma bear led them away from the road and the mob of people, into the forest, until they were out of sight. With the main attraction gone, everyone returned to their vehicles.

"Wow, I've seen bears in the wild before, but this is just as exciting as the first time!" Hug-a-Bug exclaimed.

We all hopped back into the Jeep.

"Was it a bear jam or a deer jam?" Dad asked.

"Bear jam," I answered.

Traffic began flowing again and we continued our drive north.

"When Shenandoah became a national park in 1935, there were only a few bears in the park and hardly any deer. It's really quite amazing that now Shenandoah has one of the densest populations of black bears and white tail deer in the country," Papa Lewis commented.

"Where were the bears and deer in 1935?" I asked.

"For well over two hundred years, people had made the park area home and the bear and deer population had been thinned by hunting. There were farms, pastures, orchards, grist mills, mines, and roads all throughout the park," Papa Lewis explained.

"That's so hard to believe with all this thick forest here now," Hug-a-Bug said.

"Did Indians live here in the park? I know we met the first humans that lived in the area back at Rockfish Gap. But after that period of time, did any Indian tribes live within the park area?" I asked.

"There is evidence that Indians used the park land to hunt. They've found all sorts of arrowheads throughout the park. But by the time white people settled here, the Native Americans had moved out of the area. They don't have much information on the Native Americans that once lived here," Papa Lewis explained.

Just past milepost sixty, Dad pulled off of Skyline Drive into a parking lot on the right side of the road. We had reached our destination.

"This is it. We just have a short walk to the cabin from here—less than a quarter of a mile," Papa Lewis announced.

Dad and Mom organized the gear that we would need for the night. All of us carried our packs stuffed with extra equipment: a one-burner backpack stove, water filter, food for dinner, and snacks, headlamps, reading material, and our sleeping bags. Dad and Papa Lewis carried the cooler, and we headed out of the parking lot, across the Appalachian Trail, and arrived at Pocosin Cabin minutes later. The cabin had a covered porch with a picnic table and a large stone fireplace outside the front door. Papa Lewis and Dad set the cooler down, and pulling a key from his pocket, Papa Lewis unlocked the door. We carried our gear in. There were enough bunks to sleep eight, a small kitchen area, and a wood-burning stove.

"Is this a home that belonged to a Shenandoah family?" Hug-a-Bug asked.

"No, this was built by the Civilian Conservation Corps, or CCC, in 1937 as a mountain retreat. A settler's cabin would've had the fireplace inside instead of out on the porch. The CCC was created by Franklin Delano Roosevelt in 1933 to put people to work at the height of the Great Depression. They established several camps here in Shenandoah. As a matter of fact, the very first National Park CCC camp was based here in Shenandoah. The CCC was known as Roosevelt's Tree Army. They built most of the park. Remember how I said that the people who built the A.T. had an army of help relocating it when they built Skyline Drive? That army was the CCC," Papa Lewis explained.

We stepped outside and enjoyed a great view of distant mountains from the porch. A field of wildflowers and tall grass served as the front yard of the cabin. The flowers were abuzz with bees and butterflies dipping in and out of rainbow-hued wildflowers. We were away from people and cars. It felt like our own mountain cabin home. This is awesome. The park creators sure must have thought this location through, I thought.

Papa Lewis unfolded a map and spread it out on the picnic table. "Let's take a short walk down the mountain along the Pocosin fire road to the old mission," he suggested.

"Sounds fun," I said.

"You mean there is a church mission up here in the park?" Hug-a-Bug asked.

"There was. It's no longer in use," Papa Lewis answered.

We all packed a few trail snacks, topped off our water, shouldered our packs, and set off. We walked with Papa Lewis along a path through the wildflowers and grass and came out on the fire road. The hike was just a short distance, and we dropped quite a bit in elevation. We arrived at our destination without working up a sweat.

A set of wide stone steps like what you would see in front of an official building caught my eye. What was unique about them is that they led to nothing. The steps to nowhere, I thought. I walked over to get a closer look. The steps climbed up to the rock foundation of what was once a structure of some kind. The floor, walls, and roof were gone, and all that remained was a collapsed chimney and a stone foundation overgrown with weeds and partially covered with moss. Broken glass and metal were strewn about throughout the area. An old wood frame house with a rusted metal roof stood nearby, leaning to one side, on the brink of collapse. I felt like an archeologist as we walked through the remains of these structures. You could almost feel what it must have been like to be here when this was still an active community.

"The Pocosin Mission opened in 1904 to serve the local community. An Episcopalian clergyman by the name of Fredrick William Neve moved to the U.S. from England and established several missions throughout the present-day Shenandoah National Park, with the purpose to teach religion and educate the children. Formal education was hard to come by in the deep mountain hollows of the Blue Ridge at that point in history. When Shenandoah became a park, most of the homes and buildings were torn down or dismantled. There are ruins like this throughout the park," Papa Lewis explained.

"What's a hollow? Why were the buildings removed from the park, and where did all the people go?" Hug-a-Bug asked.

"A 'hollow', pronounced 'holler' in the Appalachian region, is a term used to describe a small valley in the mountains between two hills. We will explore where the people went and what happened to the buildings later. Don't let me forget," Papa Lewis answered.

"What do you say we time travel back and see what it was like here," I suggested.

Without hesitation, everyone gathered around and I said, "Take us back to May, 1904."

A burst of air smacked us, and everything went dark then lit back up again. My backpack was gone and my hiking shorts and shirt were replaced with denim overalls and a button shirt. I held a leather-bound book entitled McGuffey's First Eclectic Reader. Hug-a-Bug wore a bright cotton dress and leather boots, and held the same leather-bound book as me. Papa Lewis and Dad wore overalls and boots, and Grandma and Mom wore dresses and boots like Hug-a-Bug's.

The stone steps that seconds ago led to nothing but crumbled ruins now climbed up to a wide double-door entrance of a building structure with a fresh coat of paint. The building looked official somehow, like it was a church or something. The tree canopy was cleared away, allowing the sun to shine down on us, and the trees sur-rounding us in the forest perimeter were massive, much larger than the trees before we time traveled.

"Bubba Jones and Hug-a-Bug, the book you're holding, the McGuffey Reader, was the book used to teach most kids to read up until the 1960s. Only one book has sold more copies than the McGuffey Reader: the Bible. So my guess is you're about to go to school. This building served as both a school and a church," Papa Lewis whispered.

The metal-roofed home that was falling into ruin before we time traveled was now a quaint, cozy little house near the mission. The front door swung open and a young woman wearing a dress similar to the one Mom had on emerged carrying a bag of books. She walked over to where we stood.

"Good morning, I'm the teacher from the mission. You must be here for school and I'm delighted to see that you even have your own McGuffey Readers. The other students are already inside if you would like to join them. Please sit with the older students towards the back," the teacher said to Hug-a-Bug and me.

"Yes ma'am," Hug-a-Bug and I said in unison as we turned to walk up the steps and into the building.

But before we climbed the steps, Dad spoke up, "Good morning. We're just visiting the area. Our kids go to school back home and will not be staying for your lesson. But thank you kindly for inviting them to join you."

"Very well, please join us for our church service on Sunday. I must get inside and teach the lesson. Have a blessed day," the teacher responded.

"Nice to meet you! You have a lovely mission here on the mountain. Thank you for opening your doors to us," Mom responded.

The teacher smiled and waved, then she turned and walked up the steps into the school.

"During this time period, children of all ages and learning levels attended school together in one- room schoolhouses like this one. Some schools had to share teachers, so school was only in session when the teacher was available. The teachers would ride on horseback from schoolhouse to schoolhouse," Papa Lewis explained in a whisper.

We all walked into the tree line, out of view, and I said "Take us back to the present."

Seconds later, a gust of air pushed me back, everything went dark, and then we were once again standing at the ruins of the Pocosin Mission, wearing our modern hiking clothes and daypacks.

"What happened to those massive trees? The trees today are so small compared to the ones back then," I said to Papa Lewis.

"In 1904, one out of every four trees in Shenandoah National Park was an American chestnut. These trees grew almost 100 feet tall and over 9 feet wide— they were huge! They were considered the redwood of the East because of their size. The American chestnut tree dominated the forests from Georgia to Maine. This tree was a huge part of the local economy in Shenandoah. Chestnuts are tasty. The nuts were collected and sold at market. The bark was peeled and sold to local tanneries to tan the leather, and it was also used to cover the outer walls of homes because it could withstand weather so well. The timber was the preferred choice of wood for making furniture, homes, and fence posts. Then in 1904, a fungus was accidentally introduced to North America from Asia. It wiped out a strand of American chestnut trees, and it spread. By 1927, the fungus had reached the Blue Ridge Mountains and killed every massive American chestnut tree in its path. The loss of this tree devastated the local economy, and this was just before the Great Depression hit. When Shenandoah became a park in 1935, the once-prominent giant American chestnuts were all dead. The park was littered with gray lifeless trees. By 1940, most mature American chestnut trees, wherever they grew, had been wiped out. Today, the American chestnut still sprouts and grows, but the fungus kills them off before they get very big," Papa Lewis explained.

"That's awful. Is there anything that can be done to bring the tree back?" I asked.

"Scientists have been working to create a tree that is resistant to the fungus by combining other tree species with the American chestnut. They are very close to introducing a hybrid species into the park. On the way back up to the cabin, let's see who's first to find a young American chestnut, untouched by the fungus. They are easy to spot if you know what you're looking for." Papa Lewis pulled out his Peterson's tree identification guide and turned to the American chestnut tree. Look for trees with green leaves that are sort of oval-shaped, with jagged edges, like what you might see on a knife. That kind of edge is called 'serrated.' The leaves alternate along the branch. The end of the branches will have flowers that grow into prickly burrs that contain chestnuts," Papa Lewis explained pointing to the picture in the identification guide.

Our focus on looking for a tree species took our mind off the short but strenuous steep climb back up to the cabin. Hug-a-Bug was the first to spot a young American chestnut tree. Before we reached the cabin, everyone had spotted at least one. Just as the cabin came into view from the trail, Dad asked me to stop. He wanted to look at something on my neck. He pulled his first aid kit out of his pack and took out a pair of tweezers. I felt a little poke in the back of my neck as he removed whatever it was.

"Bubba Jones, you had a tick on your neck just below your hairline. I got it before it penetrated your skin," Dad said.

We had been checking each other for ticks since arriving in the park. As a matter of fact, we treated our clothes with Permethrin, a chemical that is harmless to humans after it dries, but will stun and kill ticks and mosquitoes. Before each hike, we sprayed our exposed skin with bug repellent as an extra measure. Shenandoah has several species of ticks, and some of them are so small they are difficult to see. But ticks penetrate your skin and infect you with Lyme disease or Rocky Mountain Spotted Fever, both of which can be serious. The key is to prevent the tick from attaching itself to your skin and properly removing it before it penetrates the skin. Dad was on the ball!

"Thanks Dad," I said as we continued the remaining steps up to the Pocosin Cabin.

"Bubba Jones, we got a message from Washington," Hug-a-Bug yelled out to me from the porch of the cabin.

My first thought when I heard Hug-a-Bug was, He's okay! I'd been worried about Washington and his parents ever since we saw them fall off the cliff during our time travel at Blackrock. Who wouldn't be worried? Regardless of Papa Lewis reassuring us that everything was okay, it's not typical to fall off a cliff and be okay. My slow pace turned into a sprint over the remaining distance to the front porch. What did Washington's note say? What is our next mission?

THINGS ARE GETTING A LITTLE WILD

A note similar to the others that Washington had sent to us had been placed beneath a rock on the picnic table. I quickly unfolded the letter.

Dear Bubba Jones and Family,

I hope you're enjoying your time in Shenandoah National Park. I apologize for not being able to spend more time with you. I wish I could, but I'm not quite finished with my top secret project and it has required me to stay up at night. So I'm catching up on my sleep during the day. My parents thought I should reach out to you to let you know that we are all okay, just in case you were worried about us after the way we left you on our last visit. I will be in touch VERY soon with plans for us to meet again.

—Washington

"What is he up to that requires him to stay up all night? And what could be so secret that he can't share it with us?" I asked.

"Here's some exciting news," Dad interjected, "I sent a text to Uncle Boone, Aunt Walks-a-Lot, and Cousin

Crockett yesterday inviting them to join us if they can, here in Shenandoah. I haven't had a signal until now to see if they responded, but I just had a text come in from them, and guess what? They're coming up here tomorrow. Lewis, where should I tell them to meet us?"

"Tell them Big Meadows, Clark. That's where we're going from here."

"Awesome! I'm so glad they can join us!" Hug-a-Bug shouted. I was equally excited!

After Dad finished with his reply back to Uncle Boone, I borrowed his phone and sent an update to Crockett. I gave him all the details about our Shenandoah adventure and told him everything we knew about Washington's secret project. That way, I figured Crockett would have time to research anything he needed to and pack items that might help us. I wanted to find out what all of this top secret stuff was about, whether Washington was going to share it with us or not.

Our time spent corresponding with family on Dad's smartphone must have reminded Papa Lewis to turn on his phone and check for messages. He always looks out of sorts when he uses high-tech devices. He dresses in vintage 1940s clothing and wears a World War II ruck-sack—modern technology doesn't really fit in with that. He flipped up his satellite antenna and walked out into the clearing in front of the cabin. A satellite phone uses overhead satellites orbiting the earth instead of cell towers, and allows you to communicate in mountain country where cell signals are unreliable, as long as you're exposed to open sky. Papa Lewis doesn't use modern gadgets much, but when he does, he does it right. He talked for a minute with whomever was on the other end of the call, and then he folded the antenna down and put the phone back in his pack.

"The party is growing. Wild Bill is going to join us to. As a matter of fact, he's in the park right now trying to find us. He will be here soon. Put out an extra dinner plate," Papa Lewis announced.

Wild Bill, Papa Lewis's cousin, was a time traveler up until recently. He and Papa Lewis received the ability to time travel from their grandfather on a backpacking trip forty years ago. As part of the family tradition, Wild Bill had passed his time travel ability on to our cousin Crockett on our last adventure. *After being a time traveler for forty years, Wild Bill must miss having the ability to go back in time,* I thought. When we caught up to Wild Bill on our last adventure, he was using his time travel skills to retrace the steps of historic figures. He took full advantage of his time travel ability when he had it. Since we can't exactly share our time-travel adventures with just anyone, we were all pretty excited that he would be joining us.

We all went into the cabin to make sure Wild Bill had a place to sleep. We each claimed a bunk and unrolled our sleeping bags. After that, Mom, Dad, Grandma, and Papa Lewis began to assemble our meal. Hug-a-Bug and I took water duty. We gathered up our water filter and several water containers and walked down to the spring, just a short distance from the cabin. There are springs and mountain streams throughout the park that offer plenty of water sources. But even though the water looks clean and clear, it may have microscopic little things in it called protozoa. These protozoa can cause illnesses such as Giardia or Cryptosporidium. Giardia and Crypto, as it is often shortened to because it's easier to say, can make you very sick. Our filter was designed to remove these nasty pathogens. The spring was marked by a cement post just like all the other trail markers in Shenandoah, making it easy to find. Hug-a-Bug placed one end of the filter hose in the stream, and I pumped the water through our filter and out of another hose into our containers. In no time at all, all the jugs were full. We capped them, put them in a pack and climbed back up to the cabin.

Just as we reached the cabin, Wild Bill marched up from the direction of the parking lot. From a distance, he could easily be mistaken for Papa Lewis. They both wear the same 1940s era clothing and use World War II gear. Even though we had just been on an adventure with Wild Bill, so much had happened since we left him that it seemed like we hadn't seen him in ages. You'd think Wild Bill had just returned from a ten-year voyage with all the hugs, handshakes, and warm welcomes we exchanged!

We all sat down for dinner at the picnic table on the porch. Mom scooped her famous spicy camp pasta onto everyone's plates. It had a new twist this time. Papa Lewis added some of his famous dehydrated chicken to her recipe, and we were all eager to try it. Grandma passed around some dinner rolls, and Dad put out a plate of assorted vegetables. Hug-a-Bug and I set out a pitcher of lemonade we had made from the filtered spring water. The entire family pitched in to prepare this meal; Mom says that's the spirit of camping. As we ate, we caught Wild Bill up on all the action. We told him all about how

Cousin Nick, Dolly, and Washington were on some sort of secret mission, and so we hadn't been able to see much of them.

"I'm not sure what exactly the mission is that Cousin Nick, Dolly, and Washington are on, but I know who they are working for," Wild Bill responded. "After the chestnut blight hit back in the early 1900s, the government, shocked by the devastation of the forest, became concerned that something like that might happen again. They were worried about future threats to our wildlands and farmland. Another invasive fungus, non-native species, pollution, or other blight could devastate our food supply, our nation's forests and wildlands, or all three. They established a secret organization that would monitor future threats and come up with solutions. The idea was to bring the best scientists and experts together to solve problems before the damage was done."

"But why would that have to be a secret?" Hug-A-Bug asked.

"The reason for the secrecy was to prevent widespread panic over possible threats. This group has remained secret since its creation in the 1940s. Since our family mission is to protect and preserve our wildlands for future generations, joining this secret group became attractive to many members of our time-travel clan all over the country. I know, because I joined them and became a member of the group myself. Even though I'm no longer an employee, I still got regular briefings up until last year. Then the briefings suddenly ended, and I was cut out of the loop."

"We just talked about the chestnut blight today with Papa Lewis," Hug-a-Bug commented.

"Why were you cut out of the loop?" I asked.

We all sat and listened to Wild Bill, eager to learn more, while Dad struck a match and stoked a crackling fire in the stone fireplace next to us on the porch.

"When I was with the agency, we monitored threats from non-native species and other environmental concerns, and then we worked with private agencies to implement solutions to protect the native species and preserve the environment. But last year, a radical shift occurred. The climate was deemed to be a 'national security' threat, meaning that the extreme change in weather and rising sea levels could impact our national security. Since the climate had now become a government concern, our agency was called into action. The agency was instantly elevated as one of the lead covert agencies to protect our national security. Suddenly, everything the agency did became top secret. They had always operated under the radar and used codes to communicate. But now, even within the agency, information was only shared with those who had a top secret clearance. That is how I got cut out of the loop—I don't have that level of clearance," Wild Bill explained.

"Why would they want to keep this stuff secret? Wouldn't it be better if everyone knew about the problems so we could all work together to solve them?" I asked.

"When it comes to national security, there are strict protocols that must be followed, even if they seem a bit over-the-top. We don't know all the factors that make a matter confidential. That's probably the struggle Washington is having. He knows that none of us would ever leak any of his secrets, but he also doesn't want to get in trouble for breaking his sworn oath of secrecy. I agree with you, Bubba Jones, when it comes to preserving and protecting our wildlands. We all can play a role, with or without a security clearance," Wild Bill said.

"Would Washington get in any trouble if we were able to figure out what it is he is up to?" I asked.

"I suppose not as long as he hadn't given you the information. I like how you think, Bubba Jones. Maybe we can put our brainpower to work on that. In the meantime, let's enjoy our time traveling through Shenandoah and learn some more about the park," Wild Bill said.

"Sounds like a plan."

We enjoyed the sunset and then sat around the picnic table listening to Wild Bill and Papa Lewis share stories. Hug-a-Bug and I roasted marshmallows in the fireplace and made s'mores. As the fire died down, everyone started preparing for bed. I gazed into the embers of the fire. The crickets chirped their night song. The stars sparkled bright up in the night sky, and the moonlight filtered down through the trees. I was one of the last ones to go to bed. I secured the door and zipped into my sleeping bag. A cool breeze blew through the cabin's open windows, setting the stage for a great night's sleep.

Some time after drifting into a deep slumber, I woke up with my heart pounding. Had I dreamed it, or had a bloodcurdling scream awakened me? I sat up in my bunk, listening and waiting. I could see the silhouette of Hug-a-Bug sitting up, too, so I feared it had not been just a dream. There it went again—a high-pitched screech!

"W-what was that?!" Hug-a-Bug stammered.

"I don't know," I whispered.

"Oh, that's just a baby barred owl calling out to its mother. Nothing to worry about," Wild Bill said.

Hug-a-Bug let out a sigh of relief. Wild Bill's answer put our fears to bed. That's the cool thing about spending a lifetime in the outdoors like Papa Lewis and Wild Bill—they have come to know every sound in the night. I lay back down and soon sank back into a deep sleep.

The smell of bacon pulled me from my slumber. It was morning. The cabin door was open, and I could see Dad holding a sizzling skillet over our one-burner hiking stove. I got dressed and stepped outside. Beads of morning dew glistened from the grass in the morning sunlight. White-tailed deer grazed nearby, gracing us with their presence. Birds sang rich notes. It was a gorgeous mountain morning!

Wild Bill and Papa Lewis studied a park map at the picnic table while sipping their morning coffee.

"Good morning, Bubba Jones," Dad whispered.

"Morning, Dad," I replied.

Slowly, the rest of the family came outside as well. Everyone gathered at the picnic table to enjoy a delicious breakfast and to find out what was on the agenda for the day.

"Our plan is to end the day in the Big Meadows area of the park. Wild Bill and I have an interesting adventure planned along the way," Papa Lewis announced.

I couldn't wait to find out what they had in store for us. There is never a dull moment when Papa Lewis and Wild Bill get together!

CHAPTER 12

THE LAND OF THE FREE

Shortly after breakfast, we all packed up our gear, tidied up the cabin, packed out our trash, and left. It's important to take all your trash with you since there is no garbage collection service. We strolled to the parking lot to continue our adventure. The weather was on our side with blue sky and sunshine. It was still on the cool side of what promised to be a warm summer day. Wild Bill had a surprise for us when we reached the parking lot. A shiny, bright red historic vehicle sat parked next our jeep. It had a tan convertible roof and whitewall tires.

"She's a beauty, don't ya think? It's a 1933 Ford Roadster with a rumble seat. I rode her all the way up here from the Great Smoky Mountains, along the Blue Ridge Parkway. I thought it would be fun to ramble along Skyline Drive in her," Wild Bill said as he unfastened the convertible top and folded it back.

"Wow! Can we ride with you?" Hug-a-Bug implored.

"You betcha! You and Bubba Jones can ride back here in the rambler seat," Wild Bill answered as he walked around to the rear, turned a latch handle, and pulled open a stow-away seat.

Papa Lewis conferred with Dad on directions and then hopped into the passenger seat of Wild Bill's '33 Ford. We pulled out onto Skyline Drive headed north with Dad following us in the Jeep with Grandma and Mom. The wind whipped our hair in all directions as we rambled down the road. I felt like I was on a roller coaster! This was fun!

"Back in the 1930s when the park was established, owning a car was a revolutionary thing, kind of like surfing on the internet in the 1990s. Everyone wanted a car, and they wanted to take a trip somewhere fun. Driving along Skyline Drive in Shenandoah satisfied this new American desire for a travel adventure perfectly. Shenandoah National Park quickly became one of the most visited national parks," Papa Lewis explained to us.

"This was one of the cars that cruised Skyline Drive when Shenandoah National Park first came to be, and it's in mint condition," Wild Bill added.

We had only been on the road for a few miles when Wild Bill turned off of Skyline at a sign announcing Lewis Mountain. Dad pulled in behind us. We stopped along a quiet two-lane road a few hundred feet off of Skyline Drive. Everyone hopped out of the vehicles.

"I'm pretty sure this campground has a camp store. Do you mind if we stop and check? I need to stock up on a few provisions," Wild Bill said.

"No problem, Bill. We would've stayed here at Lewis Mountain Campground last night if the Pocosin Cabin was unavailable. We'll follow you to the camp store," Papa

Lewis said as we hopped back into our vehicles and drove into the campground.

We climbed back into our vehicles and drove deeper into the Lewis Mountain area. On our left, an inviting grassy field with trees and picnic tables came into view. Kids ran about playing, while grownups sat at picnic tables and socialized. We continued to drive and a row of cabins came into view off to the left with people milling about. A large one story building came into view on the right side of the road, painted in the traditional deep brown used by the national parks. It looked like a place of business. The camping area was further ahead. Wild Bill stopped his car in front of the large building and turned off the engine. Dad followed suit with the Jeep. Wild Bill hopped out, walked up to the entrance, pulled open a screen door and disappeared inside. We all hoped out of the vehicles while we waited.

"That must be the store. Wild Bill hasn't come out yet," Papa Lewis said.

Two cyclists stood next to their bikes nearby. They finished guzzling bottles of water they must have bought from the store and then hopped back on their bikes and pedaled away. Their bikes were loaded down with as much gear as a thru-hiker carries on their back.

"Skyline Drive is a popular route for long distance cyclists. Based on all that gear, it looks like they are camping along the way," Papa Lewis commented.

"That sounds like a fun adventure. I'll bet those cyclists work up big appetites, just like thru-hikers," I said.

While we waited for Wild Bill, Papa Lewis filled us in with some more park history.

"This campground was designated for blacks from 1939 until 1950. During that time, this was the only facility in the park where blacks could camp," Papa Lewis explained.

"Why would the park have a separate camping area for black people?" Hug-a-Bug asked.

"Didn't the Civil War give black people their freedom? That is not fair," I said.

"Our parks are a special place to explore and be free. But I sure wouldn't feel free if I was told I had to stay in a certain area because of the color of my skin. Sadly, at the time, the South was segregated under the Jim Crow laws, which held that black people were 'separate but equal.' Black people and white people weren't allowed to mingle at school, on buses, or in public restrooms. Black people had to drink out of separate drinking fountains than white people. This policy even showed its ugly head in Shenandoah," Papa Lewis explained.

"It's amazing how far we've come since then," I said.

Just then the screen door sprang open, and Wild Bill stepped out with a bag full of supplies and walked over to us.

"Clark, Petunia, Hug-a-Bug, and Bubba Jones, how about you all go do a spectacular hike to a fantastic view? Bear Fence is right here. It's a short trip, but it's a bit of a rock scramble. The view is worth it though. Your grandma's knees are not up for it, so she and I will ride ahead to Big Meadows with Wild Bill and check on your Uncle Boone and his family," Papa Lewis suggested.

"That sounds fun!" I responded.

Wild Bill handed Dad the the keys to the roadster, saying, "How about you take her for a spin this time?" Dad's face lit up like that of a little boy on Christmas morning. He hopped in the car, followed by Mom, Hug-a-Bug, and me. Wild Bill, Grandma, and Papa Lewis motored off in the Jeep.

We drove along Skyline Drive for a little over a mile then, Dad turned off of the road into the Bear Fence Mountain parking lot. The four of us got out and pulled our packs on. Since it was a rock scramble, we left our trekking poles in the car so our hands would be free. We reviewed the map and it showed a 1.2-mile loop. We crossed the road and a short distance in, the trail intersected the A.T. We stopped to check our maps.

"Hey, Hug-a-Bug, Bubba Jones!" a familiar voice shouted.

It was Soul Search, one of the three thru-hikers. I introduced him to our parents. They felt like they already knew him after hearing our stories. He told us that he had stayed at High Top Hut last night. Bagel Man and Fungus were further ahead, and they all were hiking to Big Meadows today. We shared that we were planning to stay at Big Meadows, too. We invited Soul Search to join us on our Bear Fence loop. He declined, saying that he would have a great view all day, and he wanted to remain focused on the A.T. He continued on, and we continued following the Bear Fence loop.

Further on, the trail became steep and rocky, then the rocks gave way to huge boulders. We climbed slowly using our hands as well as our feet. Occasionally, Dad reached back to take Hug-a-Bug's hand to help her along. In a short while, we reached the summit.

"Wow! I feel like I'm on top of the world!" I shouted.

We stood on a jagged rock with a 360-degree view. We could see distant mountains and blue sky with wisps of cotton candy clouds all around.

"I see why Papa Lewis likes this hike. It's beautiful up here," Hug-a-Bug said.

"It sure is. Honey, why didn't we ever hike this trail before?" Mom asked Dad. Mom and Dad explored parts of Shenandoah National Park on their honeymoon years ago.

"We hiked up to a different peak further north. Remember? We had spectacular views there, too," Dad replied.

"Oh, I do remember. Let's make sure we visit that peak with the kids while we're here."

"Sounds like a plan."

We each broke out a granola bar and our water, before slowly working our way back down the mountain. The terrain evened out once again, and we soon arrived back at the car.

"That was fun," Hug-a-Bug grinned as she took off her pack and climbed into the rambler seat. We all whole-heartedly agreed. Dad started up the old Ford and we pulled out onto Skyline Drive towards the Big Meadows area. Excitement brewed, knowing we were about to join up with more family. Crockett will help me uncover Washington's secret, I thought as we rolled down the road.

WHAT'S THE BIG DEAL?

W e drove along Skyline Drive for a short while. Every so often we would slow down to wait for a deer to get out of the road. I noticed a cement post marking a trail off in the tree line and then I noticed a white blaze - the A.T. marker - painted on a tree. Another white blaze was painted on a tree across the road indicating that the trail crossed Skyline Drive.

"Papa Lewis was telling me that the Appalachian Trail crosses Skyline Drive twenty-eight times in Shenandoah," Dad commented as we continued driving. "We're entering the part of the park known as the Central District. This is where most of the park visitors spend their time because there is so much to do here: hiking, horseback riding, fishing, camping, birding, and much more. The Central District contains the park's two main lodges, Skyland and Big Meadows, along with several cabins at Lewis Mountain. Two of the four park campgrounds are located in the Central District as well: Lewis Mountain and Big Meadows, where we are headed right now."

The tree canopy on the right side of the road gave way to blue sky, cotton ball clouds, and an expansive relatively flat field of grass, an unusual sight on the top of a mountain. A sign came into view announcing Big Meadows. We turned left off Skyline Drive and immediately passed a gas station. Next to the gas station was the Big Meadows Wayside, similar to the one down at Loft Mountain where we had blackberry milkshakes. The road then skirted along to the right and led to a parking area and the National Park Byrd Visitor Center.

"We will explore all of this later. Right now the plan is to check the bulletin board at the Big Meadows campground. That is where everyone was told to post a note."

"Why don't we just call them?" Hug-a-Bug asked.

"A lot of times when you are in the mountains, you can't get cell phone coverage. Sometimes, since you're in the wilderness, there isn't a nearby tower, or if there is a tower, mountains or heavy tree canopy can actually block cell signals. Plus, we kind of come up here to 'get away from it all,' and that includes technology. Using cell phones or other gadgets kind of takes away from the experience of getting back to nature." Dad explained.

As we drove slowly towards the campground, we saw people walking along a path that paralleled the road. They smiled and waved to us, and we waved back. This continued all the way into the campground.

"I think Wild Bill's car is drawing lots of attention," Hug-a-Bug observed with a smile.

We came to a stop behind a big RV. We all stepped out of the car and walked ahead to the campground's ranger station. A Dutch door served as the registration counter for campers to check in. A park ranger in full uniform was giving out information to some campers. Off to the left side of the counter an array of notes and messages were posted on the wall for campers. One of them was addressed to the Lewis and Clark clan.

"This must be for us," I said, pulling the note off the board and unfolding it. It read, "We're at campsites E173 & E 175."

We hopped back into the old Ford Rambler and followed the "E" campground signs. This was a huge campground, but each section was clearly marked and easy to navigate. It was the height of summer, and nearly every site was occupied. We saw our Jeep parked in a shaded area next to our tent at campsite E175, and we immediately recognized our cousin Crockett and his parents, Uncle Boone and Aunt Walks-a-Lot, next to us in campsite E173.

Hug-a-Bug and I hopped out of the car and ran over to greet the new addition to our Shenandoah adventure crew. Mom, Dad, Papa Lewis, Grandma, and Wild Bill converged on Uncle Boone, Aunt Walks-a-Lot, and Crockett. For several minutes there was hugging, kissing, and catching up on all the family news. Then Papa Lewis announced a surprise for our Mom and Dad.

"You two have a room at Big Meadows Lodge tonight. It's on us. We know you stayed there on your honeymoon and thought you might enjoy revisiting it."

Mom and Dad hugged Papa Lewis and Grandma for their generosity.

"Thank you, Mom and Lewis."

"It's our pleasure, Clark. The lodge is close enough to walk, but you might want to drive up to drop off your gear. Why don't you two go get settled in your room, then come back down, and we can make plans for dinner," Papa Lewis suggested.

"Sounds great. See you guys in a bit," Mom responded, as she and Dad hopped into the Jeep and motored out of camp.

"Bubba Jones and Hug-a-Bug, this note was left on the bulletin board for you when we arrived to set up camp," Papa Lewis said as he handed me the note.

It had to be from Washington! I quickly unfolded it and Hug-a-Bug and Crockett leaned in to read along with me:

I look forward to meeting the additional family, especially Crockett! Decode the message below and meet us at that location tomorrow. See you soon!

—Washington

OXMFAXK   ZXJM   YOLTK   ELRPB   MLOZE

LZQLYBO   PFU   KLLK   KFKBQBBK   BKQV
KFKB

I unfolded the cipher and the plain text decoder sheet from earlier and went through each group of letters.

Plain	A	B	C	D	E	F	G	H	I	J	K	L	M
Cipher	X	Y	Z	A	B	C	D	E	F	G	H	I	J

Plain	N	O	P	Q	R	S	T	U	V	W	X	Y	Z
Cipher	K	L	M	N	O	P	Q	R	S	T	U	V	W

This was the message I deciphered:

Plain: RAPIDAN   CAMP   BROWN   HOUSE PORCH

Cipher: OXMFAXK   ZXJM   YOLTK   ELRPB MLOZE

Plain: OCTOBER   SIX   NOON   NINETEEN TWENTY   NINE

Cipher: LZQLYBO   PFU   KLLK   KFKBQBBK QTBKQV   KFKB

I showed Papa Lewis the message.

"I was going to recommend that we visit Rapidan Camp. It's one of my favorite spots in the park," Papa Lewis said.

"What is Rapidan Camp?" I asked.

"When Herbert Hoover was president, from 1929 to 1933, he used Rapidan Camp as the presidential retreat. It was only when FDR became president that the presidential retreat was moved to its current location, Camp David," Papa Lewis explained.

"Wow! We're going to meet up with another president!" Hug-a-Bug said excitedly.

"Not only the president, but the first lady, Lou Henry Hoover, and whomever else is there, too," Papa Lewis explained.

"Maybe Washington's secret mission has something to do with the president. After all, presidents know a lot of secrets," I suggested.

"Well, let's see what Washington shares tomorrow. If he doesn't reveal what's going on, I have a plan," Crockettt shared.

"I knew we could count on you, Crockett," I replied.

While we waited for Mom and Dad to return from the lodge, Hug-a-Bug sat down at the picnic table to update her timeline. Uncle Boone and Aunt Walks-a-Lot went back over to their campsite to finish setting up camp. As Hug-a-Bug was working, Papa Lewis handed her the Shenandoah Junior Ranger Booklet.

"I picked this up at the Byrd Visitor Center for you," Papa Lewis said.

"Thanks Papa Lewis. Just what I wanted, so I can become a Shenandoah Junior Ranger while we're here," Hug-a-Bug said, smiling.

"Bubba Jones, before we got on the road, I printed the Ranger Explorer Activity Guide for us. I found it on the National Park Service website. It's for ages thirteen and up," Crockett said, handing me the Guide.

"Wow, you really did do your homework, Crockett," I said as I leafed through the Guide.

Crockett and I sat with Hug-a-Bug and found the Rapidan Camp on the Central District map. As we were sitting there, a hiker walked by just ten yards away from our camp. She was wearing a full backpack and using trekking poles. Then I noticed a white blaze on a tree above her head. We were camped next to the Appalachian Trail! Hug-a-Bug got excited when she saw a female thru-hiker. She jumped up from the picnic table and ran over to greet the woman. They talked for several minutes, and then Hug-a-Bug led the hiker into our camp.

"Everyone, this is Ginger. Her two other friends, Cinnamon and Garlic, already passed by. They started hiking the trail in May, down in Georgia. They've hiked through Tennessee, North Carolina, and almost all of

Virginia. They are going to do a flip-flop. When they get to Harpers Ferry, they are going to catch a ride up to Mount Katahdin in Maine and hike south back to Harpers Ferry so they won't have to worry about the weather. They're staying at Blackrock Hut tonight," Hug-a-Bug said

"Wow, Hug-a-Bug. I couldn't have explained it better myself," Ginger said.

We all greeted Ginger, then Uncle Boone led her over to his camp and had her pick whatever food she wanted from his supply. Ginger wasn't shy—she scooped up several Snickers bars and energy bars. Aunt Walks-a-Lot made a ham and cheese sandwich for Ginger, which Ginger wolfed down in about three bites. "Thanks a bunch for the trail magic, but I need to catch up to my trail family at Blackrock Hut," Ginger said as she turned to go, striding off down the trail.

"What did she mean by 'trail magic'?" Aunt Walks-a-Lot asked.

"Trail magic is any act of kindness or generosity shown to thru-hikers by people along the trail. And the people who provide trail magic are called trail angels," Papa Lewis explained.

"I can't wait until I'm old enough to hike the A.T.!" Hug-a-Bug responded.

Just then, Mom and Dad strolled into our campsite.

"Hey guys, why don't we all eat at the Big Meadows Lodge? It's just a short walk. We can cut through the picnic area," Dad suggested.

Everyone liked that idea. We locked all of our food and scented items in our vehicles to keep from attracting animals. The campground had several reported bear sightings, making it all the more important to properly secure our food and anything else that a bear might find attractive.

We followed Mom and Dad through the picnic area, then followed a footpath up a small hill. The trail led us onto a grassy green lawn, where we followed a circular driveway leading up to the lodge. The building was a sprawling structure of wood and stone, with a massive stone chimney. It looked warm, rustic, and inviting. Now this, I thought, is a lodge!

"This lodge was built by the Civilian Conservation Corps in 1939. They used stone from this area, and the wood is all American chestnut," Papa Lewis said as we walked into the lobby. A guest counter stood off to the right, with a lodge employee checking in new guests. A line of people stood by the dining area, waiting for a table to become available.

"I put our name in for a table before we returned to the campground, anticipating that you would all want to eat here," Mom said.

We followed Mom and Dad through a set of French doors into a large airy room. The walls and ceiling were made of American chestnut stained to reveal the natural wood grain. The room had a vaulted ceiling supported by large wood trusses. A massive floor-to-ceiling stone fireplace dominated one end of the room. French doors to the right of the fireplace led out onto a stone terrace. Huge rustic chandeliers suspended by chains hung from the ceiling. The entire back wall of the room was windows, allowing natural light to flood the room and providing a beautiful view of the Shenandoah Valley. Logs popped and crackled in the fireplace, and cool air drifted through the French doors on the opposite side of the room.

"This is known as the Great Room," Papa Lewis told us.

It had a feeling of greatness to it. It was large, but cozy—the perfect place to hide from the elements and take in the mountain vista.

"Lewis and Clark, your table is ready," A woman called into the great room from the lobby.

The woman led us to our table. As our group walked through the dining room something caught my attention out of the corner of my eye. I looked to my left and caught a quick glimpse of Washington, walking away from the guest services counter and out the front door.

"It's Washington!" I exclaimed, turning to run outside to catch up to him. When I got outside, he was nowhere in sight. There were people everywhere, getting in and out of vehicles, walking past, standing and talking. The distant parking lot was bustling with vehicles pulling in and out of parking spots. A large tourist bus idled in front of the gift shop. But no Washington.

"What's going on?" Crockett shouted from behind me.

"I swear I saw Washington, but now he's gone," I answered.

"Don't worry Bubba Jones, we'll get to the bottom of this," Crockett assured me.

We went back inside and found our seats in the dining room for a table of ten. It had the same cozy rustic feel as the great room. Food service staff zipped back and forth carrying platters of steamy food. The air was filled with the sounds of social chatter and the metallic clink of forks and knives. No need to time travel to get the feel of what life was like here in the past: the decor had been restored to the 1930s era. Even the menu had historical food choices. Best of all, they had blackberry ice cream for dessert. We walked out of the dining room with full stomachs. We said good night to Mom and Dad, and walked back to the campground for the night. We all sat around the fire until the sun set, then we all turned in for the night at about the same time. We had a big day in store for us tomorrow. We were going to get to the bottom of this secret mission!

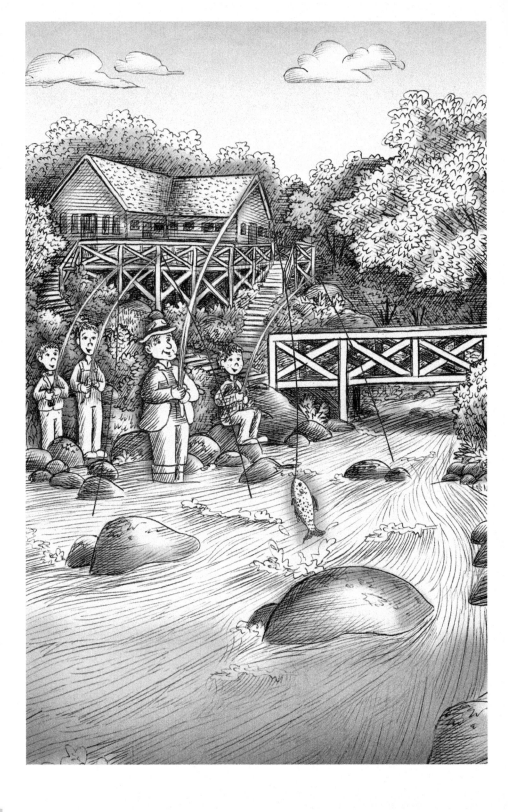

PRESIDENTIAL DOUBLE HEADER

In the morning, Papa Lewis, Wild Bill, Uncle Boone, Aunt Walks-a-Lot, and Grandma all managed to gather outside under the dining canopy without waking us. It was only the rich aroma of freshly brewed coffee that woke Crockett, Hug-a-Bug, and me. We all dressed for the day's hike and joined the others outside. Grandma put out granola bars and a bowl of fruit for breakfast.

"I figured we would keep it simple this morning," Grandma said, referring to breakfast.

We all thanked Grandma for breakfast and dug in.

"I'm looking forward to visiting Rapidan Camp. That's been on my time-travel bucket list for a long time," Wild Bill said with a smile.

After everyone was finished eating, Papa Lewis unfolded a map to review the plan.

"We will park at Milam Gap, just before milepost fifty-three on Skyline Drive, and take the Mill Prong Trail. That's just a few miles from here. The hike is four miles round trip to Rapidan Camp and back," Papa Lewis said, while dragging his finger along the route on the map. "We should pack along some lunch and have a picnic while we're there."

Grandma and Aunt Walks-a-Lot started an assembly line of bread, deli meat, cheese, condiments, carrot sticks, and energy bars for everyone's lunch. Mom and Dad showed up as we were packing our lunches.

"Good morning, everyone," Dad said with a smile.

"The strangest thing happened this morning on our walk across the parking lot to eat breakfast at the lodge. We saw Cousin Nick, Dolly, and Washington pull into a parking space. They got out of the car loaded down with all sorts of hiking equipment, as if they had been out all night. They disappeared into one of the lodge rooms before we could catch up to them," Mom said, looking perplexed.

"That is odd. Why would they hike at night?" I asked.

"I have a theory. Let's see how today goes, and if I still think I'm right, I'll share it with all of you," Crockett said.

We all climbed in our vehicles and drove out of the campground. In minutes, we arrived at the parking lot across from the trailhead. We shouldered our packs, crossed the road, and started down the trail toward Rapidan Camp. The hike was pleasant. We followed a gradual downgrade most of the way. At one point, we crossed a stream—one of three—that required some careful rock hopping, but other than that, the hike was pretty tame. The trail opened up to a fire road which circled Rapidan Camp. A national park building came into view as we entered the camp.

"That's the Creel Cabin, one of three original structures built when President Hoover used this as a presidential retreat. The original complex had thirteen buildings spread out to blend in with the natural surroundings. All but three—the Creel Cabin, the Prime Minister's Cabin, and the Brown House—were in disrepair and torn down. The original buildings were all connected by gravel paths, much like the one we're on now," Papa Lewis explained.

We followed Papa Lewis along a narrow path through a stand of trees which opened up to a clearing in view of a green-roofed one-story cabin. It was the same brown as all of the national park buildings, with massive stone chimneys on the end walls.

"President Hoover was elected in 1928, and in 1929 the Great Depression hit. People lost their jobs and their homes. Businesses closed, and people struggled to simply find food and shelter. Hoover was wrongly blamed for the Depression even though he had nothing to do with it. He wanted a place to retreat from the hectic presidential life in Washington. He believed that in order to make sound decisions, you needed to have a place to relax and rejuvenate, both mentally and physically. He found the sound of rushing water to be very relaxing. After he was elected, his aides searched for a retreat with three features: it had to be within one hundred miles of D.C. for easy access, it had to be at an elevation of at least 2,500 feet, and it had to offer good fishing. Fishing was one of President Hoover's favorite pasttimes. Some advocates for the creation of Shenandoah National Park thought having the presidential retreat there would bolster their plans. They promoted this location, and the Hoovers liked it. First Lady Lou Henry Hoover oversaw the creation of Rapidan Camp. The Hoovers turned down government funds to build Rapidan. They were very wealthy and paid for the construction out of their own pockets. They did agree to have the Marines provide the labor and build the camp."

Gesturing toward the cabin, Papa Lewis said, "This is the Brown House, where The Hoovers stayed and entertained guests. It was built where two streams come together to form the Rapidan River. We're supposed to meet Washington and his parents there in just a few minutes." Pointing to another cabin, Papa Lewis said, "That is the Prime Minister Cabin, where the Prime Minister of England stayed when he visited," Papa Lewis explained, pointing to another building a short walk from the Brown House.

We followed Papa Lewis up onto the back porch of the Brown House. A park volunteer was speaking to a group of tourists and about to lead them inside and give them a tour. I could hear the sound of rushing water. I walked to the far end of the porch and found the source: the Rapidan River was just feet off of the back porch.

When the tour group stepped inside, my family gathered together in a circle. I held the family journal tight with one hand and said, "Take us back to twelve noon, October 6, 1929."

A gust of wind blew and everything went dark. I blinked my eyes and it was daylight once again. Our surroundings had changed: the forest around us abounded with old growth Eastern Hemlocks and some American chestnut trees. Our clothes had changed; Crockett and I wore denim bib overalls, button down shirts, straw hats, and well-worn shoes—we were dressed like the mountain boys of that era.

"Hey, Bubba Jones, you made it," a familiar voice shouted from the river bank.

It was Washington with Cousin Nick and Dolly. We walked down to greet them at the bank. They, too, were dressed like the locals. Washington looked tired. So did Cousin Nick and Dolly. They all had dark circles under their eyes.

"That's President Hoover fishing over there," Washington said, pointing to a man further downstream dressed in a wide brim hat, a dark suit coat, a tie, and fishing waders. Several men dressed in suits stood nearby.

That sure is a fancy fishing outfit, I thought.

"Mrs. Hoover is inside the cabin. If you're asked, say we live on the other side of the mountain. We're just out for a stroll," Washington advised.

Just then, a woman with short white hair and wearing a dress appeared on the porch, and smiled at us.

"Would you lovely ladies like to join me for tea?" she asked.

"That's Mrs. Hoover. This is your chance to mingle with the first lady," Papa Lewis whispered to the ladies.

"That would be wonderful," Grandma replied as Aunt Walks-a-Lot, Mom, Grandma and Hug-a-Bug climbed the porch steps and went inside the cabin with the first lady of the United States.

President Hoover took notice of us watching him. He walked along the bank towards us.

"I have some extra rods and tackle if you boys would care to join me. I'm just enjoying some downtime until my next meeting with Prime Minister MacDonald. We need to talk about our Navies," President Hoover confided.

"We would love to join you," Dad said.

A member of President Hoover's security detail walked away and reappeared with fishing gear for us. For the next half hour, we tried our best to catch some brook trout with the president of the United States. President Hoover was good at this—he caught several.

"I love spending time out here. It clears my head and reinvigorates me," President Hoover told us.

We heard an airplane engine overhead, and minutes later, a low-flying prop plane zipped above us.

"That's my mail. That will keep me busy for a while when it arrives," President Hoover said.

The plane dropped a mailbag further up the mountain, and a short while later, I saw a U.S. Marine in full dress uniform carry the mailbag up to the Brown House.

"I guess I better head in and go through my mail before my meeting. Nice meeting you fellows. Enjoy the rest of your time at Rapidan. If you stick around, we're going to have a steak cookout at the fire pit tonight," President Hoover said.

"Thank you, Mr. President. You sure are a good fisherman," Crockett said.

"Thank you, young man," President Hoover said as he turned to go. He waved and walked away towards the Brown House. Minutes later, the ladies in our group reappeared on the porch. They thanked the first lady for tea, then walked down the porch steps and joined us.

"Wasn't that great?" Washington asked.

"I like First Lady Hoover. Instead of sitting inside the cabin, Mrs. Hoover led us outside to a wooded area for tea and then on a short walk around the grounds. She told us that she camped and fished when she was a kid. And she sure knows a lot about the rocks and plants. She shared all sorts of interesting facts about the woods. She even offered to take us on a horseback ride up the mountain later," Hug-a-Bug said.

"Mrs. Hoover was the first female to graduate with a degree in Geology from Stanford. She loved the outdoors. She was also very involved with the Girl Scouts and served as the Girl Scout president. The Hoovers started a school to serve the families in the area and Mrs. Hoover was very involved with that," Papa Lewis explained.

"She sure was a go-getter," Mom said.

"I have one more presidential trip to take you on. You will need to meet me up in the field at Big Meadows. Here's a note with the specifics," Washington said as he handed me a folded piece of paper.

"Washington, does the presidential time traveling have anything to do with your secret mission?" I asked.

"No, Bubba Jones. I just thought it would be cool to meet the president," Washington answered with a grin.

"You look like you're not getting enough sleep. Have you been performing your secret mission at night?" Crockett asked, furrowing his brow.

"We've been working late into the night, Crockett. I can't tell you on what though. It's classified. I'm almost done though, and then I'll be able to spend more time with you guys," Washington answered.

Cousin Nick, Dolly, and Washington walked down the trail and soon were out of sight. Moments later, we heard a KABOOM, which told us they had returned to the present. We walked down the same trail, formed a circle when we were out of view of the camp, and returned to the present. We followed the trail back to our vehicles. When we arrived, I unfolded Washington's note:

Bubba Jones, here's one more adventure for the day. See you soon! Decode the message to find out where to meet.

YFD JBXALTP CFBIA XRDRPQ QTBICQE KFKBQBBK QEOBB BIBSBK XJ

Your cousin, Washington"

I pulled out my cipher key:

Plain	A	B	C	D	E	F	G	H	I	J	K	L	M
Cipher	X	Y	Z	A	B	C	D	E	F	G	H	I	J

Plain	N	O	P	Q	R	S	T	U	V	W	X	Y	Z
Cipher	K	L	M	N	O	P	Q	R	S	T	U	V	W

This is what I decoded:

Plain: BIG MEADOWS FIELD AUGUST TWELFTH NINETEEN THIRTY THREE ELEVEN AM

Cipher: YFD JBXALTP CFBIA XRDRPQ QTBICQE KFKBQBBK QEFOQV QEOBB BIBSBK XJ

Everyone gathered around to see.

"That's just a few minutes up the road, with no hiking required. Based on the year and date, that will put us right in the middle of a Civilian Conservation Corps camp, Camp Fechner, NP-2. That's the date President Franklin Delano Roosevelt (FDR) visited the camp. FDR won the election against President Hoover and took office while the U.S. was in the middle of the Great Depression.

FDR created the CCC to help put the country back to work again. Shenandoah was home to some of the first national park CCC camps. The CCC built this park. At one point, there were over one thousand CCC men here in Shenandoah. They planted trees, removed old structures, cleared the dead American chestnut trees, and built the campgrounds, lodges, cabins, shelters, and many of the roads. The CCC was a huge success for FDR. The program continued until World War Two broke out. With the war, the nation's focus shifted, and the number of CCC boys dropped," Papa Lewis said.

We all hopped in our vehicles and motored north to Big Meadows. When we reached the clearing, we pulled into a parking lot on the edge of Big Meadows. We got out of our cars and walked along a gravel road up into the meadow.

"Bubba Jones, do you mind if I take the lead on this time-travel adventure?" Crockett asked me.

"You got it, Crockett," I replied.

We stopped walking when we were sure we were out of view of others, and then we formed a circle.

"Take us back to August 12, 1933 at 11:00 a.m.," Crockett said.

A gust of wind blew me back. Everything went dark, and seconds later it was daylight once again. All of us guys wore what appeared to be military pants, shirts, and ties. The women wore nice dresses. Old-fashioned cars lined Skyline Drive, and across the meadow, I could see rows of one-story buildings similar to what you would see on a military post. Hundreds of people were gathered near the buildings. Scanning the crowd, I spotted

Washington, Dolly, and Cousin Nick standing together nearby wearing the same type of clothing as us.

"Two presidents in one day! Are you ready to meet FDR?" Washington asked us.

"You bet!" Hug-a-Bug answered.

All of us walked across the meadow together. I thought this would be a good time to ask Washington one last time about his secret mission, and about his nighttime activities.

"My parents said they saw you and your parents pull up at Big Meadows Lodge at breakfast time, and you were unloading gear as if you had just returned from a hike. Were you out all night?" I asked Washington.

"I can't explain any details about that, Bubba Jones. I may have already told you too much. I'm sorry," Washington responded.

We were approaching the crowd of people, so I let the conversation drop. There were no women, just men, so I hoped that our family wouldn't draw too much attention. A line of black convertible 1930 Packards were parked in a line along Skyline Drive.

"That's the presidential motorcade. FDR is having lunch with the CCC boys today. See all the people with cameras? FDR is showing off the CCC program to the media," Washington explained.

I recognized FDR immediately. He was seated at the end of a long table, eating and talking with the CCC boys. He was dressed in a suit and tie and was seated in the biggest, nicest chair at the table. FDR was flanked on either side by important looking men in suits, and Secret Service agents stood nearby. The CCC boys sat along both sides of the long table with FDR, wearing military-style uniforms. They laughed and talked as they passed bowls of food around the table. It was a homestyle meal of chicken, mashed potatoes, corn, and sliced bread. FDR gave a short speech, remarking on how good life was for the CCC boys.

"The CCC was one of FDR's most successful programs. It gave young men across the nation a chance to work, learn new skills, and provide their families with some income. The camps were run by the Army, which is why they wore uniforms and lived in barracks. During their downtime, the CCC boys learned to read and to carve wood, and were taught many other skills as well," Papa Lewis explained. "They also had time to play sports— some pretty rousing football games, for sure!"

The ladies in our group must have led the organizers to believe we were part of the presidential party, because a CCC boy led us to a table, seated us, and brought us bowls of food. We ate a scrumptious meal. When we finished eating, we stood up, slipped through the crowd, and made our way across the field and out of sight.

"That was awesome having lunch with the president and the CCC boys," I said.

"FDR returned here once again on July 3, 1936 to dedicate Shenandoah as a National Park," Papa Lewis added.

"I have just one more day of work, and then I should be done with my secret mission. There is plenty for you to do here until I wrap it up," Washington said.

"What would happen if we discovered what your secret mission is? What would your secret agency do?" Crockett asked.

"I'm not sure. That most likely wouldn't happen, though. Give me until tomorrow evening, and I'll be done," Washington said as he walked away with Cousin Nick and Dolly. Seconds later, we heard a loud bang, and they were gone.

We formed a circle and Crockett said, "Take us back to the present."

The next moment, we were standing in the meadow, but the CCC boys and the barracks were gone. Instead, photographers and birders weaved through the field, snapping pictures of the birds, deer, wild flowers, butter-flies, and wildlife.

"Good job on the time-travel trip," I said to Crockett.

"Thank you, Bubba Jones. You heard Washington - he has just one day of work left on his secret mission. We have to act fast if we want to catch him at work. I'm pretty sure I know what he's doing. What do you say we go back to camp, and I'll show you my plan?" Crockett said.

"Can we go to the Byrd Visitor Center first? I want to get sworn in as a Junior Ranger," Hug-a-Bug said.

"The visitor center has a park museum and a theatre. How about we all go and check it out?" Dad suggested.

Everyone agreed, so we piled into our cars and drove over to the visitor center. A bronze statue of a shirtless CCC boy stood to the left of the main entrance.

"That's Iron Mike. He was placed there in commem-oration of all that the CCC did here in the park," Papa Lewis explained.

We all went in to explore. Dad and Mom walked with Hug-a-Bug over to a large counter with several park rang-ers and volunteers standing by ready to help. The rest of us sat down in the theatre to watch a video about the park. Afterward, we all wandered through an exhibit on the history of the park. It was so well done that I thought for sure we had time traveled right there in the exhibit. Many of the places in the park that we had time traveled to were included in the display. We emerged from the exhibit just in time to see Hug-a-Bug being sworn in as an official Shenandoah Junior Park Ranger. Stopping in the gift shop, Mom picked out some post cards while Dad leafed through some books. I approached Dad and looked over his shoulder to see what he was looking at. "This looks like it has some good tips. I think I'll get it for my sister. I keep inviting her to come on these trips with us, but she says it wouldn't work with her kids being so young," Dad commented.

"Oh yeah? What's the book?" I asked.

Dad flipped the book closed to show me the cover: Get Your Kids Hiking. A blurb in the top corner of the cover read, "How to start them young and keep it fun."

"Sounds perfect, Dad!"

After Mom and Dad made their purchases, we left the visitor center and headed back to camp. It was time to get to the bottom of Washington's secret.

CHAPTER 15

NOT SO SECRET ANYMORE

"**Y**ou can't pass by the Big Meadows Wayside without stopping in for a blackberry milkshake," Dad reasoned as we left the visitor center, which just happened to be right next to the Wayside. No one argued and we all strolled over to the restaurant. Several groups of thru-hikers sat at picnic tables. Making our way through them, we stepped into the Wayside to get some ice cream. Hug-a-Bug and I tried a chocolate and vanilla swirl cone this time, while everyone else went for a blackberry milkshake. We struck up a conversation with a group of hikers. They were southbounders. They had walked all the way from Mount Katahdin, Maine through New Hampshire, Vermont, Connecticut, New York, New Jersey, Pennsylvania, Maryland, and West Virginia—over twelve hundred miles. They were accompanied by a section hiker who had joined them in Front Royal, the town at the north end of Shenandoah. The section hiker was planning to hike the entire Shenandoah section of the A.T. and end at Waynesboro, the town at the south end of the park. Dad offered to treat them all to some ice cream, and they eagerly accepted. Finishing our ice cream, we wished the hikers well and headed back to camp. It was time to find out what Crockett's plan was.

When we got back to camp, Hug-a-Bug and I sat down at the picnic table with Crockett to go over his theory.

"When you told me that Washington was on a mission in Shenandoah working for a secret agency, I figured it must be to monitor something in the park. I started thinking about what could be so important that a government agency would want to keep it secret. I started with a search of non-native species in the park—you know, plants or animals that are in the park that don't belong here. The park website reported over 350 non-native species in the park. Many of these are plants introduced by early settlers that don't cause any harm. But some non-native species do pose a risk because they damage or kill the native species. According to the park website, some of these high-risk non-native invasive species include: the gypsy moths, which kills trees; the hemlock woolly adelgid, which kills the hemlock trees; the European starling, which competes for the habitat of the indigenous birds; and the kudzu vine, which chokes out native plants. The park has a policy in place to control and manage these infestations," Crockett explained, handing me the article he printed from the park website.

"I was also thinking about what other animals or plants in the park might need monitoring. With a little research, I came up with the peregrine falcon, the fastest bird in the world. The falcon almost became extinct from DDT, a pesticide used on crops. DDT caused the peregrines' egg shells to become so thin that many eggs would break long before the developing baby birds inside were ready to hatch. With such a high rate of egg breakage, the peregrine falcon population plummeted. DDT has been banned for decades now, and peregrines are making a comeback in Shenandoah. They are being carefully monitored," Crockett explained, handing me another article he had printed from the Shenandoah Park website.

"But I don't think Washington is monitoring any of these things," Crockett stated.

"Then what is he doing?" I asked.

"Are you ready? Drum roll, please," Crockett said as he pulled out a stack of articles. "When you told me that Washington was working at night, that got me thinking. What would you monitor at night?"

"Something nocturnal," I suggested.

"Exactly," Crockett stated as he shuffled through the stack of articles and pulled one out.

"He's monitoring the Shenandoah salamander, scientific name Plethodon Shenandoah," Crockett said as he handed me a fact sheet.

"Are you saying this is all about a salamander?" Hug-a-Bug asked, looking highly doubtful.

"The Shenandoah salamander only lives in the Shenandoah, it's on the Fish and Wildlife Service Endangered Species list, and it's nocturnal," Crockett explained.

"Why would this be considered so secret that Washington couldn't share it with us?" I asked.

"Look at this, Bubba Jones," Crockett said as he handed me a stack of articles.

The first article was titled, "Climate Change Deemed Growing Security Threat by Military Researchers."

The second article said, "Pentagon Signals Security Risks of Climate Change."

The third article was titled, "Climate Change Comes to Shenandoah."

The fourth article said, "Saving Salamanders in Shenandoah."

"Scientists think the Shenandoah salamander may disappear completely due to the effects of climate change. Bubba Jones, the government has determined that climate change is a national security risk. Even the Pentagon and CIA are involved," Crockett explained.

"Of course! Why didn't I think of that? When the government classified climate change as a national security risk, Washington must have been instantly activated by the secret agency he works for because he's an expert on the Shenandoah, and this was now a matter of national security. Wow, Crockett, nice job!" I stated.

"How could a tiny little salamander be a matter of national security?" Hug-a-Bug asked, still clearly in disbelief.

Our parents and grandparents were listening in on this whole conversation and reading the articles that Crockett found.

"Crockett, I used to work for the agency that Washington is working for. I believe you are right on track," Wild Bill chimed in.

"Hug-a-Bug, every species that disappears is a big deal. Every animal is a part of the food chain and ecosystem. If one species disappears, others will be affected. Since the salamanders are already endangered, and we are monitoring their numbers, we would notice if their population dropped, and we could investigate whether climate change was responsible. If it was, then the salamanders would have tipped us off that other species are also likely to be affected by climate change. This is most likely why Washington and his parents were activated to monitor the Shenandoah salamander," Papa Lewis explained.

"Crockett, you said you had a plan. What is it?" I asked.

Everyone was focused on Crockett. He pulled out another article.

"The only place in the entire world the Shenandoah salamander is known to exist is on three mountaintops right here in the park. All three mountain tops are north of Big Meadows. One of them is really close, maybe four miles at most to the trailhead. We could split up and head out to all three areas tonight and catch Washington doing his research. He will most likely be on one of these mountains," Washington explained.

"My guess is that he's currently working on Hawksbill since that is so close to Big Meadows Lodge where they're staying. The other two mountain peaks are closer to Skyland, so he would probably stay there if he was working on those mountains," I suggested.

"We checked with the front desk, and Crockett and his family have not checked out of Big Meadows. Hiking at night can be dangerous, especially on top of mountains with steep cliffs. I think we should stick together. Why don't we do something in this area until nightfall and then follow their vehicle when they leave. Your mom and

I saw them get out of their car. We know which one it is," Dad suggested.

"That's a great idea. I'd like to show you guys a really stunning waterfall and some local history while we're at Big Meadows. Who's in?" Papa Lewis asked.

Grandma, Mom, and Dad decided to stay at the lodge and watch for Washington, Cousin Nick, and Dolly to leave. The rest of us decided to go with Papa Lewis. Papa Lewis gave Mom and Dad a second satellite phone to contact us if anything happened. We packed some sandwiches, snacks, and extra batteries for our headlamps— it could be a long night. Papa Lewis planned to lead us down to Dark Hollow Falls, then pick up the Rose River Trail and hike to Fishers Gap. We dropped Uncle Boone's and Aunt Walks-a-Lot's vehicle at Fishers Gap, then we all crammed into Wild Bill's old Ford and drove back to the Dark Hollow Falls trailhead. From there, we were off to see the waterfall.

The trail was very steep. It twisted back and forth over switchbacks, dramatically descending the mountain for about an eighth of a mile before dropping us at Dark Hollow Falls. It was amazing! We stood by the edge of a pool of water at the bottom of a seventy-foot waterfall cascading over a rocky cliff. We took in the sight for a few minutes, and then Papa Lewis led us further down the trail. We continued on a steep descent, following a surging stream all the way down to a trail junction. An old metal bridge, wide enough to support a vehicle, crossed over the stream. We followed Papa Lewis over the bridge and onto the Rose River Trail for a short distance until he stopped and pointed out a cement column with steel rods protruding from it.

"Back in 1845, this was a copper mine. It was mined on and off up until the early 1900s. The shafts are all filled in now. There used to be several mines in the park."

"Any gold mines out here?" Hug-a-Bug asked.

"No gold mines, Hug-a-Bug," Papa Lewis answered.

We retraced our footsteps back over the old bridge and took up the Rose River Fire Road. The trail was wide enough for a vehicle and not as steep as the trail we had followed down the mountain. Papa Lewis stopped near where a trail met the road.

"Follow me," Papa Lewis said as he led us onto the side trail.

In a few yards, we came onto a sign announcing "Cave Cemetery."

"Shenandoah National Park has over one hundred cemeteries left from when this land was privately owned. This is one of them, and it's still in use. Most of the cemeteries are inaccessible by car. But the fire road allows access for families to continue to bury their loved ones here," Papa Lewis explained.

We walked among the gravestones. Some of them dated back to the civil war. Others were more recent and had flower arrangements propped against the stones.

It's a very peaceful place to be laid to rest, I thought.

When we exited the cemetery, Papa Lewis checked his satellite phone for word from Dad. Seeing that he had a message, he walked out into a clearing and dialed up his voicemail. A minute later, he folded the satellite antenna and walked back over to us.

"They're following Washington, Cousin Nick, and Dolly out onto Skyline Drive going north. They are going to leave another message when they reach the destination. We better hike back to Fishers Gap and get ready to join them," Papa Lewis said.

We all had more pep in our step as we hiked the Rose River Fire Road up to Fishers Gap, completing the hike while it was still daylight.

"This fire road used to be a turnpike that crossed over the mountain at Fishers Gap. Stonewall Jackson used this road to cross his army over the mountain in November of 1862 to support troops at Richmond," Papa Lewis explained.

We reached Fishers Gap and Papa Lewis had another message from Dad, saying they had followed Washington, Cousin Nick, and Dolly to the Upper Hawksbill parking area just a few miles north of us. Papa Lewis let Dad know we were on our way. We all piled into the vehicle, and Uncle Boone drove us to Upper Hawksbill. We saw the Jeep and pulled in next to it. Dad hopped out of the Jeep and explained that Washington, Cousin Nick, and Dolly had no idea that Mom and Dad had followed them. Washington and his parents had gotten out of their car, grabbed a bunch of gear from the trunk, and headed up the Upper Hawksbill Trail just minutes ago.

"Everyone, pack along your wind parka and fleece. At 4,050 feet above sea level, Hawksbill is the highest mountain in Shenandoah. When the sun goes down, it might get cold up there, even in the summer. It's just a little over a mile to the top, and it's rated easy to moderate. There is a great spot to eat dinner and watch the sunset at Byrds Nest Shelter Two." Papa Lewis told us.

"What do we say when we run into them?" I asked

"Whatever comes to mind, Bubba Jones," Papa Lewis answered.

Our team of ten followed the trail up towards Hawksbill. The trees changed the higher we climbed. Balsam fir and red spruce, trees usually found further north, up in Maine and Canada, marked the landscape as we neared the summit. The Byrds Nest Shelter Two came into view and there were people milling about everywhere. We stopped at the shelter to rest, and that's when we realized all the people up here weren't just here for the gorgeous sunset we were now admiring from the highest mountain in the park - they were hard at work. We all scrambled towards the talus slopes to get a closer look, and that's when we discovered Washington, Cousin Nick, and Dolly working with a whole team of people.

"Washington, what's going on?" I asked.

"Hey, Bubba Jones, I didn't expect to run into you guys up here. I was going to bring everyone up here tomorrow and show you what we're working on," Washington replied.

"Why has this been such a secret?" I asked.

"Bubba Jones, I honestly don't know why I have to keep everything so secret. That's the orders from the agency I work for. Trust me though, the agency shares the same vision and mission as our family: to preserve our parks and wildlands for future generations. I want to show you some exciting things going on right here, and it's no secret—at least not anymore. This is what I was going to show you tomorrow. Shenandoah National Park is home to fourteen species of salamanders. One of them, the Shenandoah salamander, is in danger of becoming extinct, so it's protected as a federal endangered species," Washington Explained.

While Washington was talking, Crockett took off his pack and pulled some information he had printed from the park website, along with a few other articles.

"We've learned a lot about the Shenandoah salamander," Crockett said, handing Washington the articles. "The park website says that salamanders are amphibians, and they breathe through their skin. They're nocturnal, so you won't see them during the day. They live in just three small mountaintop areas in the park where it's cooler than other areas. They eat bugs, and they live in moist, shaded soil beneath the rocks up on these talus slopes."

"Wow, Crockett, you really did your homework!" Washington said.

"That's how we found you. You were spotted in the Big Meadows Lodge parking lot returning from a night in the woods, so we guessed that you were researching something nocturnal. Since the Shenandoah salamander is nocturnal and endangered, we figured that might be what you were studying. I also found these articles about how climate change could impact the Shenandoah salamander, and some of the articles linked climate change to national security. At that point, I figured that was why your secret agency activated you—since climate change has become a matter of national security, your mission was to study the salamander to see if it was being impacted by climate change. Because if it was, then our national security might be in jeopardy," Crockett explained.

"Looks like you figured it out! Some of the most fragile species can help scientists learn what to expect from a changing climate. With their numbers already so low that they are an endangered species, the Shenandoah salamander could be completely wiped out. Scientists believe it was pushed out of other areas in the park to just these three mountains by the red-backed salamander. They are also looking into the human impact on the Shenandoah salamander. Just about everyone up here is either a scientist or a zoologist. They are here to help the park try to save the Shenandoah salamander," Washington explained.

"What is a zoologist?" Hub-a-Bug asked.

"A zoologist is a scientist that studies animals and their behavior," Washington answered.

We watched the team of experts at work as they measured spaces between rocks, took pictures, and recorded information. They looked serious, and they looked like they knew what they were doing.

"So, does this mean that you can join us for the rest of our adventure?" Hug-a-Bug asked.

"Yes! I've wanted to do that all along—this mission was unexpected. We received word today that it's no longer classified," Washington explained.

"What's classified mean?" Hug-a-Bug asked.

"If information is classified, I can't share the information with anyone unless I have permission from my agency," Washington answered.

Washington continued, "When we informed the agency that a team of scientists and national park staff were already hard at work trying to save the Shenandoah Salamander, they declassified our Shenandoah Salamander mission so we could partner with the scientists and the park to help out. The agency made an exception to its rules and determined that it would be in the best interest of our national security if we all work together and inform everyone about the endangered Shenandoah Salamander. And by the looks of it, this team up here has things under control."

"So that means no more secret messages?" Crockett asked.

"No more secret messages," Washington confirmed.

"Do you want to plan some more adventures in the park together, Washington?" I asked.

Washington looked over to Cousin Nick and Dolly. They both smiled and nodded.

"Yes, I would like that, and boy, do I have some places in the park you've got to explore!" Washington said with enthusiasm.

"I reminded the agency that Washington is just a kid. I also let them know that some relatives have joined us in the park and we would like to spend some time visiting," Cousin Nick explained.

We sat up on the rocks along the edge of the mountain and enjoyed the sunset while we ate our dinner. Afterward, Washington, Cousin Nick, and Dolly packed up their equipment, and we all trekked back down the mountain.

We were all excited that Washington, Cousin Nick, and Dolly would be able to join us for the rest of our Shenandoah adventure.

CHAPTER 16

WHAT AN AMAZING ADVENTURE

We made plans to meet back at our campsite for s'mores. We were all exhausted, but we were excited to finally be able to spend some time with Washington, Cousin Nick, and Dolly without having to decode a message or travel back in time! As the fire died down, and the s'more supply dwindled, we decided to wait until morning to make adventure plans. We said goodnight and tucked in for a good night's rest.

The next morning was the first morning since we arrived in the park that everyone slept in. Everyone except for Hug-a-Bug, that is. She was up and out at the picnic table at first light to update her timeline. Eventually, everyone was up and about. Wild Bill took his turn at meal preparation and fried up some bacon and scrambled eggs. We sat enjoying the stillness of the morning. Deer wandered through the campground, birds sang in the trees, and a lone hiker quietly passed by our little campsite nestled along the A.T.

Shortly after breakfast, Washington and his parents, and Mom and Dad came down from the lodge to join us.

Within minutes, the picnic table was covered with maps as Washington, Cousin Nick, and Dolly shared some of their adventure ideas. We were, after all, right in their backyard. Plans were made to move our base camp north to Skyland for a few days and then some of us would cap off our Shenandoah adventure with an overnight hike on Old Rag Mountain.

We went about the business of breaking camp and packing up. In a short time, we were all loaded into our three-vehicle motorcade, driving north on Skyline Drive.

Skyland, a mountaintop resort lodge with a bird's eye view of the valley below, was only about eight miles away; we arrived there in minutes. We pulled up in front of the guest check-in area, and Cousin Nick went in to arrange rooms for all of us. A dining room and gift shop were right next door, and people sat on a terrace between the two buildings, reading books, socializing, and enjoying the mountaintop view. Nick returned to his car, and we followed him down a quiet lane that opened up to a sprawling complex with several cabins, a conference hall, and two-story buildings. We located our adjoining rooms, keyed in and dropped our gear inside, then met back outside to go explore.

Washington, Cousin Nick, and Dolly led us up to an old rustic two-story building on a hillside, set apart from the rest of the complex. It looked nothing like the other buildings. It was made of stone and wood, and the walls were covered in tree bark instead of siding. Log railings enclosed the porch and a small upper deck.

"That's a different-looking building," Hug-a-Bug pointed out.

"That's Massanutten Lodge. It was built in 1911, years before this was a park. A man by the name of George Pollock inherited the land from his father's mining business and started a resort here in 1894. He called it Stony Man Camp. Mr. Pollock's wife, Addie Nairn Hunter, had this cabin built by an architect who was well-known at the time. Pollock advertised his new resort to well-to-do city folks as a refreshing place to vacation. People came up here from Washington D.C., and other cities to escape the summer heat and enjoy the cool mountain air. The camp started out with just simple tent structures. The

Massanutten Lodge looks like it's open for visitors. Let's go in," Cousin Nick said.

We entered the building through a second level door and found a park ranger inside ready to answer our questions. The lodge had been restored and furnished to what it was like when Addie Nairn Hunter lived here. The inner walls of the two rooms were all wood and both the living room and bedroom had a rustic stone fireplace. The windows and doors were open allowing a gentle breeze to blow in through the screen. The living room had bookshelves throughout crammed with old hardbound books and an old upright piano filled one side of the room.

"Mrs. Pollock was a classical pianist. She came from a wealthy family and moved here from D.C. She was divorced when she met George Pollock. She had this lodge built before she remarried to Mr. Pollock. Let me know if you have any questions," The Park Ranger said.

"Thank you," Mom said as we continued to walk through the home.

The bedroom, adjacent to the living room, had a 'Women of Skyland' exhibit which caught all of our attention with some very impressive ladies that spent time here during an era long gone.

For the next half an hour we discovered that George Pollock's mom, Louise Plessner Pollock, who spent a lot of time at Skyland, played a big role in the creation of kindergarten. Another notable guest, Mary Johnston, was the bestselling author of a 1900 book, *To Have and to Hold*. We learned that Mrs. Pollock was very independent and loved nature. She even bought land near the present day Limber Lost Trail near Skyland in an effort to save some old growth trees from the logger's ax. We exited the building with a new found flavor for the woman and culture of Skyland.

We regrouped outside and Washington suggested what we were all thinking. "What do you say we visit Stony Man Camp?"

"You read my mind," I said.

We all gathered in a circle behind a stand of trees.

"Take us back to July 7, 1899," Washington stated.

A gust of wind blew us backward and everything went dark. Seconds later, the wind died down, and we found ourselves standing between rows of large canvas house-like tents built on top of wooden platforms. Our clothing had transformed into formal wear. All of the males in our family wore suit jackets and ties, while Hug-a-Bug and the women all wore fancy dresses. Horses were tied to hitching posts outside of each tent. Other men and women, also well-dressed, sat under trees and on rocks, reading books and talking. A loud blast from a horn startled all of us.

"What was that?" Crockett asked in a whisper.

"Let's go and see for ourselves," Washington suggested.

We walked to the top of the hill, and there stood a man wearing a large Mexican sombrero and Spanish-style clothing. He held a bugle to his lips, which explained the horn blast we had heard.

"Why is that man dressed in Mexican clothing blowing a horn?" Hug-a-Bug asked.

"That's George Pollock. I've always wanted to meet this very eccentric man. From what I've read, he was very creative in entertaining his guests. He used his bugle to call his guests to lunch and to wake them in the morning. They didn't have wake-up calls or alarm clocks back then. I would guess he's dressed like that to entertain the guests," Wild Bill said before walking over and introducing himself to George Pollock.

We followed the rest of the guests into the dining tent and sat down to a scrumptious meal of fresh garden vegetables and meat stew. After lunch, Mr. Pollock asked everyone to gather outside and he led us up to Stony Man, just a short walk from the camp. I was dripping in sweat wearing so much clothing, and I could see beads of sweat on the others' faces, too, as we trekked up the mountain. It was worth it, though. When we reached the top, we were treated to an unbelievable view of the Shenandoah Valley below. Knowing this was one of the three remaining mountain peaks where the Shenandoah salamander could be found in modern times, I kept my eyes peeled for a possible sighting. While the group sat and enjoyed the view, Mr. Pollock broke out in song to entertain his guests. Afterward, we all hiked back down to the camp.

In our absence, a horse-drawn stagecoach had arrived with new guests. Mr. Pollock greeted them and reviewed the agenda for the evening and the next day.

"After you get settled in, we will have a nice meal with vegetables fresh from our mountain garden, and we'll have some live entertainment to dance to by some local mountain men. Tomorrow morning, we are going to enjoy a dip in the waters of White Oak Canyon," Mr. Pollock shared.

We slipped away between a row of tents, out of view, formed a circle, and Washington brought us back to the present. I felt much more comfortable without the tie and jacket. The tents were gone, and we were standing near the old Massanutten Lodge once again.

"Mr. Pollock sold plots of land to wealthy and famous people who replaced the tents with cabins. The Byrd's, a Virginia family that was very involved in politics, owned a cabin here called the Byrds Nest. As a matter of fact, the Byrds Nest cabin is still here—not to be confused with the Byrds Nest shelters in the park. The Harry F. Byrd Visitor Center is named after a member of their family. Mr. Pollock hosted the Southern Appalachian National Park Committee here in 1924. He figured that he would be allowed to stay and run his resort if this became a park, but that's not what happened. Instead, when this area did become a park, a new concessionaire was brought in to run all the lodging, and the private owners were forced to sell," Cousin Nick explained.

"The Shenandoah National Park Association was established in the summer of 1925 to raise funds for the Commonwealth of Virginia to buy land and help advocate to make this a park. In 1926, President Coolidge signed a bill to create Shenandoah National Park. Harry F. Byrd, a wealthy governor of Virginia and an avid Shenandoah enthusiast, used his political connections to promote the creation of the park. Then in 1928, the Commonwealth of Virginia approved the Park Condemnation Act, which gave the state the authority to buy everyone's land through what is known as eminent domain. At that time, residents were allowed to stay on their land, and for four years after that, while President Hoover was president, people were allowed to stay. But when FDR became president, all of the land owners were forced to sell their homes and farms and move out of the park; only a few were allowed to remain due to special circumstances. This forced over four hundred and fifty families out of their homes," Papa Lewis added.

"The government can make you move out of your house? That would be horrible," I said.

"Yes, it was very upsetting to many of the mountain people. Some of them had been here for several generations. Some of them tried to fight the forced removal through the courts, but lost. Two men, Ferdinand Zerkel and William Carson, were instrumental in overseeing the park's creation," Papa Lewis explained.

"Nearly all of the homes were destroyed when this became a park. At the time, they were not considered of historic value. In the fall and winter, when the leaves have fallen, you can see some of the old stone chimneys and foundation remains of some of the homesteads," Cousin Nick added.

"I'm so glad this is a park. It's so beautiful here, and Shenandoah does fulfill George Pollock's idea of providing a refreshing getaway from city life. But it's sad that it came at the expense of the people that once called this their home," Dolly said as tears filled her eyes.

"Shortly after the idea to create the park became a reality, the Great Depression hit, and the donations to make this a park dwindled. Due to the lack of funds, the original vision to buy over 500,000 acres was scaled back. Today, the park is 200,000 acres, less than half of the original plan. That is why the present-day boundary looks so jagged and the park itself is so narrow. Shenandoah is surrounded on all sides by private land," Cousin Nick told us.

I looked at the park map, and now it made sense why the park's perimeter was so irregular.

"Would you like to see my favorite view up on Mary's Rock?" Washington asked. "It's not far—just a short hike."

We were all interested in seeing the view, so we went back to our rooms, grabbed our gear, hopped in our vehicles, and drove north to the Meadow Springs parking area. From there, we took the Meadow Springs Trail to the summit. The climb was steep at times, but when we reached the summit, it was all worth it. I felt like I was on top of the world! We had a 360-degree view of the Piedmont on the east, the Shenandoah Valley on the west, and a bird's-eye view looking down at Skyline Drive. We posed for a group photo, and then I sat down to quietly take it all in for a few minutes. I could see why this was Washington's favorite spot.

"This is the peak we hiked up to on our honeymoon," Mom said as she squeezed Dad's hand and enjoyed the memory.

The next day was the start of our big overnight hike. We assembled all the necessary gear.

Bubba Jones, Papa Lewis, and Hug-a-Bug's Backpacking Gear List

Tent

Sleeping bag

Sleeping pad

Backpack

Cooking pot

Spoon

Mug for hot beverages

Hydration hose system and/or BPA free bottles

Water filter or treatment system

Rope, 50 feet (to hang bear bag)

First-aid kit

Pack cover

Whistle

Duct tape (two feet for emergency repairs)

Compass

Map / Topography Map

Magnifying lens or glasses to read map

GPS

Signal mirror

Water

Food (enough for three meals each day, plus snacks, and an extra day of food for emergency use)

Tooth brush

Toothpaste

Hand sanitizer

Wet wipes

Biodegradable soap

Toilet paper

Personal hygiene products

Bandanna

Vitamins

Head lamp/flashlight

Watch

Sealable waterproof bags (to keep gear & clothes in)

Sunscreen

Sunglasses

Hiking poles

Bug repellent (DEET or Picardin)	Survival / locking blade knife
Plastic spade shovel (for digging your cat hole)	Stove (one burner backpack stove)
Camera	First aid medicine
Paper/pen	Clothing (non-cotton)
Book	Layers of synthetics, wool, fleece and waterproof breathable outer shell
Repair kits	
Batteries	
Cell phone & charger	Dress for the weather conditions.
Park emergency phone number	Bring extra sets of clothes.
Matches and lighter	**Base Layer**
Swiss army knife or multipurpose knife	Underwear (2–3 pairs)
	T-shirts (2–3)
	Socks (2–3 pairs)

Mom, Dad, Grandma, and Dolly dropped us off at the Nicholson Hollow Trail, then continued north on Skyline Drive to set up camp at Mathews Arm Campground, where we would spend our last night together in the park. Our plan was to hike down to one of the few remaining settler cabins, Corbin Cabin, and then camp along the Hughes River. Tomorrow, we would hike over Old Rag and Dad would pick us up in the parking area. Starting down the trail, we descended the mountain for a few miles beneath the shade of thick forest. The trail leveled off into a hollow. Off to the left, rocks were piled neatly in a line next to the trail. It was what was left of a perimeter fence from back when this was a farm. We crossed a stream, and a cabin came into view.

"That's Corbin Cabin. It was built by George Corbin in 1910. He was a relative of the Nicholsons that lived in this hollow. It's one of the few homes that wasn't destroyed. As a matter of fact, it's one of the PATC cabins that you can rent," Cousin Nick explained.

Without a word being said, we were all thinking the same thing: Let's go back in time.

We gathered around Washington and he said, "Take us back to 1910."

A gust of air smacked us. Everything went dark and then lit back up again. We were all wearing overalls and straw hats, with the exception of Hug-a-Bug, who wore a calico dress. Pear, apple, peach, and cherry trees filled a small orchard near the cabin. A man was busy splitting firewood near the porch, and a woman was hanging clothes on a clothesline to dry. Chickens clucked from a small coop nearby, and pigs squealed in a pen.

The man noticed us and stopped his work. It was George Corbin. "You all must be lost. Can I help you find your way?" he offered.

"Thank you kindly. We're heading towards Old Rag Mountain. Sorry to disturb you. Have a good day," Cousin Nick answered.

George Corbin pointed in an eastward direction towards a trail and said, "Old Rag is that way."

"Thank you," Papa Lewis replied as we all walked past the Corbin Cabin in single file.

When we got out of view, Washington brought us back to the present, and we continued hiking until late in the day, only stopping for lunch and a few snacks. We spent a tranquil night along the Hughes River. The next morning, we got up at sunrise, enjoyed breakfast, and tackled Old Rag. It was the hardest hike I had ever done! We had to hoist each other up in some spots. We squeezed through deep, narrow, granite crevices, and scrambled up and over massive boulders. The Bear Fence Hike was a good practice run for this, and the view at the summit did not disappoint! The view at the top looked over the eastern mountains with a 360-degree view in every direction was the best. We sat and drank in the beauty for a while before hiking back. We reached the parking lot, where we met Dad right on schedule. We had conquered the most difficult hike in the park!

"You guys should be very proud of yourselves. That was one rugged trail, and you did it!" Papa Lewis said to us as Dad steered the car out of the parking lot.

For the next few days, we explored the North District of the park together. We toured an old CCC camp across the road from Mathews Campground. Some of the buildings were still standing, giving us a really good feel for what the camp was like back in the day. There were so many more historical artifacts in the park that we still hadn't seen.

We took a short hike near Compton Peak to see a spectacular columnar joint formation, created millions of years ago as lava cooled and formed into the six-sided geometric columns. On the way back to the vehicles, we ran into Soul Search, Bagel Man, and Fungus. They were headed to Front Royal, at the northern end of the park. They planned on continuing north on the A.T. to see how far they could get before winter.

Wild Bill requested that we stop at the Dickey Ridge Visitor Center before leaving the park. En route on Skyline Drive, Nick asked us to pull over. We pulled into a parking lot, and Nick jumped out of the lead vehicle.

"That mountain range over there is Massanutten. See the northern tip of the mountain? That's called Signal Knob. During the Civil War, the Confederates, and sometimes the Union, used that point to send signals about each other's movements," Cousin Nick explained.

We got back in our cars and drove on. We arrived at the Dickey Ridge Visitor Center, and Wild Bill insisted that we time travel back to the summer of 1938. Crockett did the honors, taking us back to July of 1938. Everything went dark and lit up again, and as with our last time travel experience, we were all wearing formal clothes. The ladies wore 1940s-style dresses and the men wore jackets and ties. A band was playing music on an outdoor patio, and people were dancing. Old model cars were parked everywhere, and cabins stood nearby.

"They used to have dances up here," Wild Bill told us before turning to Mom and asking, "Petunia, may I have this dance?"

She smiled, and the two of them walked over to the terrace and did the foxtrot. Dad danced with Grandma. Papa Lewis danced with Dolly. Then they all switched dance partners for a few songs before Crockett brought us back to the present.

We took a short hike across the road to the Snead Farm, an old apple orchard and farm. The homestead was long gone, but the barn was still standing and in good condition. No need to time travel here. As we explored the grounds, we found the old spring, walked along the foundation of the home, and peeked into the barn. We could feel what it must have been like to live here when the Snead family worked the farm. After a bit of exploring, we walked back to the visitor center.

On the last night before we would go our separate ways, we cooked one of my favorite camp meals - campfire pizzas and s'mores for dessert. We reminisced about our adventures. We felt like we had really explored Shenandoah National Park. But Washington pointed out that we had hiked only a sampling of the five hundred miles of trails, and there were many more artifacts and sights to see. We simply couldn't do it all in one trip. So it was decided that we would plan another adventure. Wild Bill, Cousin Nick, and Papa Lewis capped off the night with the song "Oh Shenandoah." Campers all around us joined in to sing along.

The next morning, everyone was up early. Dad and Mom brewed the coffee, and we had a simple breakfast of granola bars and fruit. Then we all worked together to break camp. In a short time, we had crammed all of our gear either into the back of our Jeep or on the roof. The goodbye ritual of hugging, kissing, and promises to write or call began. Wild Bill was headed back to Tennessee; Cousin Crockett, Uncle Boone, and Aunt Walks-a-Lot back to Georgia; Washington, Cousin Nick, and Dolly to Charlottesville, and my family back to Ohio. We were about to hop in the Jeep, when a campground host rode up in a golf cart.

"Are you the Lewis and Clark gang? Does someone in your group go by the name of Bubba Jones?" the campground host asked.

"That's me," I replied, wondering what this was about.

"This is for you," the campground host said as he handed me an envelope.

"Thank you," I called out to him as he drove away.

"That's not from me," Washington commented as I opened the letter.

Dear Bubba Jones and Time-Travel Family,

You will find a key to decode the message below in your mail when you get home. The message will lead you to your next park adventure.

Sincerely,

A Long-Lost Relative

We all stared at each other, wide-eyed and grinning, knowing that another adventure awaited.

The End.

Hug-a-Bug's Timeline

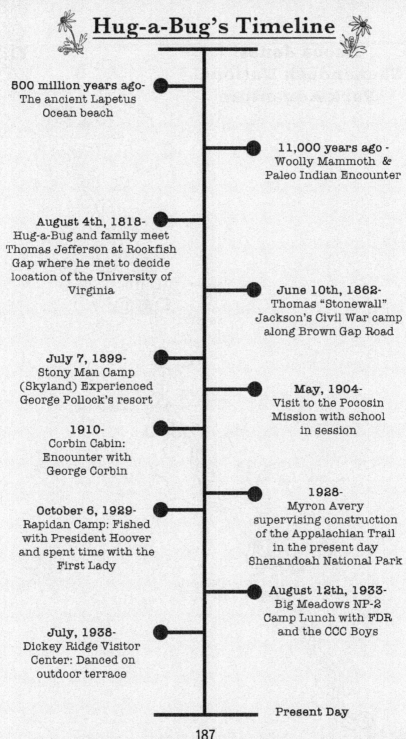

500 million years ago-
The ancient Lapetus
Ocean beach

11,000 years ago -
Woolly Mammoth &
Paleo Indian Encounter

August 4th, 1818-
Hug-a-Bug and family meet
Thomas Jefferson at Rockfish
Gap where he met to decide
location of the University of
Virginia

June 10th, 1862-
Thomas "Stonewall"
Jackson's Civil War camp
along Brown Gap Road

July 7, 1899-
Stony Man Camp
(Skyland) Experienced
George Pollock's resort

May, 1904-
Visit to the Pocosin
Mission with school
in session

1910-
Corbin Cabin:
Encounter with
George Corbin

1928-
Myron Avery
supervising construction
of the Appalachian Trail
in the present day
Shenandoah National Park

October 6, 1929-
Rapidan Camp: Fished
with President Hoover
and spent time with the
First Lady

August 12th, 1933-
Big Meadows NP-2
Camp Lunch with FDR
and the CCC Boys

July, 1938-
Dickey Ridge Visitor
Center: Danced on
outdoor terrace

Present Day

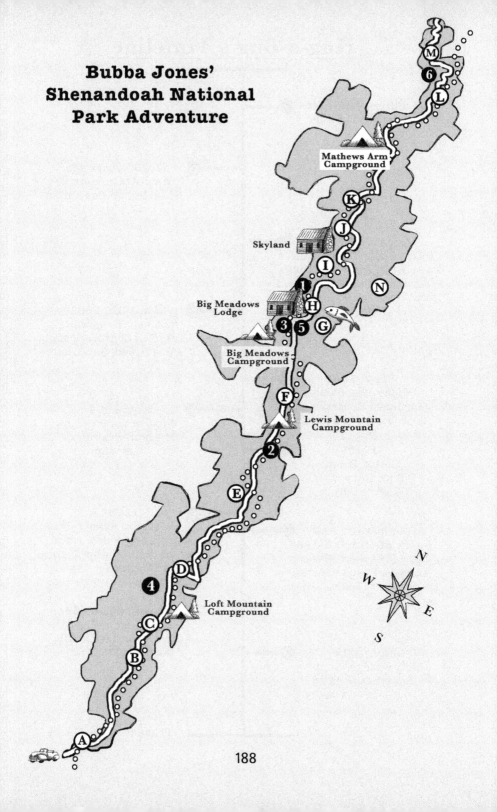

Bubba Jones'
Shenandoah National
Park Adventure

Mathews Arm
Campground

Skyland

Big Meadows
Lodge

Big Meadows
Campground

Lewis Mountain
Campground

Loft Mountain
Campground

N
W E
S

Hiking Trips

(A) Appalachian Trail from Rockfish Gap to Beagle Gap: Start at Rock Fish Gap and hike north to Beagle Gap Milepost 105 to Mile 99.5

(B) Calvary Rocks: Milepost 90. Rip Rap Trail Parking.

(C) Blackrock (South District) Mile 84.8.

(D) Doyles River Falls: Mile 81.1.

(E) Pocosin Mission site: Mile 59.5.

(F) Bearfence: Mile 56.4.

(G) Rapidan Camp via Mill Prong Trail: Milam Gap Parking area Mile 52.8.

(H) Dark Hollow Falls to Fischer Gap Via the Rose River Fire Road & Trail. Start at Mile 50.7 and end at Mile 49.5.

(I) Hawksbill Mountain: Mile 46.7.

(J) Stony Man Trail: Mile 41.7

(K) Marys Rock: Mile 31.6

(L) Columnar joint formation- Near Compton Peak: Mile 10.3

(M) Snead Farm Trail Mile 5.1

(N) Old Rag Mountain & Corbin Cabin via the Nicholson Hollow Trail

Places Visited

❶ Massanutten Lodge

❷ PATC Pocosin Cabin

❸ Byrd Visitor Center

❹ Loft Mountain Wayside

❺ Big Meadows Wayside

❻ Dickey Ridge Visitor Center

Activities

o o o   Appalachian Trail

Campgrounds

Fishing with Hoover

Lodges

Skyline Drive

Curriculum Guide

The Adventures of Bubba Jones is recommended for grades 3-7 and may be a helpful resources for several curriculum topics.

Math
Cipher Code/ Problem Solving

Social Studies
National Parks
Paleo Indians
Southern Appalachian Culture
Mountain Cultures
Civil War
Lewis & Clark
American Presidents: Hoover, Jefferson, FDR
Appalachian Trail
Civilian Conservation Corps.

Science
Endangered Species/ Shenandoah Salamander
Climate Change
Geology/ Ancient rocks, oceans, and mountains
non-native species
Chestnut blight
Peregrine Falcon
DDT

Wooly Mammoth
bear
deer
Barred Owl

The Adventures of Bubba Jones
Discussion Questions

Chapter 1: Is this Shenandoah National Park?

1. Can you list 2 of Shenandoah National Park's most famous features?

2. What are woolly mammoths? And why do they no longer exist?

3. Why did the Paleo Indians move from place to place?

4. What prank does Bubba Jones pull on Hug-a-Bug?

Chapter 2: Action at Rockfish Gap

1. What are the rules of time travel that Bubba Jones (Tommy) must follow?

2. Who was Thomas Jefferson? And what is he famous for? Why is he meeting with James Madison and James Monroe?

Chapter 3: Secret in the Mail

1. Where did Bubba Jones receive the 2nd half of the coded message? Who gave it to him?

2. Who else used this cipher system? What was their passcode?

Chapter 4: The People Behind the Trail

1. How far had the thru-hikers that Hug-a-Bug met already hiked? What states had they traveled through?

2. What does PATC stand for? What does this group do?

3. Who was Myron Avery? How is he different from Earl Schaffer and Grandma Gatewood?

Chapter 5: A Night on the Mountain

1. How many campgrounds does Shenandoah National Park have? And which one is Bubba Jones' family using?

2. How does Nick use his time traveling abilities?

3. Where is Bubba Jones headed next?

4. Who did Bubba Jones and Hug-a-Bug suspect was behind the code that led them to Shenandoah?

Chapter 6: A Civil War Rendezvous

1. Who was Thomas "Stonewall" Jackson? How did he use the Blue Ridge Mountains during the Civil War?

2. What was the Civil War fought over? Which side, Union or Confederacy, won the war?

Chapter 7: The Cipher Master Revealed

1. Why does Nick believe it's dangerous to tell anyone else about their time traveling abilities?

2. How did Washington become the youngest employee of Nick's top secret agency?

Chapter 8: If These Rocks Could Talk

1. What are skolithos linearis. And how are they made?

2. What caused large rocks to break apart and form a talus slope?

3. Why didn't Washington give Bubba Jones a new cipher?

Chapter 9: A Blackberry Mood

1. What are the three thru-hikers' nicknames?

2. What happened to the original old-growth forest? And what is protecting the current second-growth forest?

3. Are apple trees native to Shenandoah?

Chapter 10: From One Mission to Another

1. What was Papa Lewis' advice about bear safety?

2. What was school like in 1904? How is that different from what school is like today?

3. How were the American chestnut trees affected by a fungus in 1904? What are scientists doing to help these trees?

Chapter 11: Things are Getting a Little Wild

1. What illnesses can you contract from drinking water with protozoa? How does Bubba Jones collect clean water?

2. What is Washington's secret group working to avoid?

Chapter 12: The Land of the Free

1. What made Shenandoah one of the most visited national parks in the 1930s?

2. What were the Jim Crow laws? And how did they affect Shenandoah?

Chapter 13: What's the Big Deal?

1. List some things park visitors can do in the Central district.

2. What was Rapidan Camp used from from 1929-1933?

3. What is trail magic?

Chapter 14: Presidential Double Header

1. What were the 3 necessary features of the presidential retreat?

2. List 3 facts about Mrs. Hoover.

3. What is Iron Mike?

Chapter 15: Not So Secret Anymore

1. What is Crockett's theory?

2. Why is it a big deal if a single species disappears?

3. List 5 facts about the Shenandoah salamander.

Chapter 16: What an Amazing Adventure

1. Who was George Pollock?

2. What parts did President Coolidge, Harry F. Byrd, and the Commonwealth of Virginia play in the creation of Shenandoah National Park?

3. Why is the park's perimeter so irregular?

Bibliography

Unitied States. Appalachian Trail Conservancy. Accessed September 27, 2015. http://www.appalachiantrail.org/

Allen, Thomas B. George Washington Spymaster: *How the Americans Outspied the British and Won the Revolutionary War*, Washington, D.C: National Geographic Society, 2004.

Anderson, Larry. *Benton MacKaye: Conservationist, Planner, and Creator of the Appalachian Trail*, Baltimore, MD: John Hopkins University Press, 2002.

Alt, Jeff. *The Adventures of Bubba Jones: Time Traveling Through the Great Smoky Mountains*, New York City, NY, Beaufort Books Publishers, 2015.

Alt, Jeff. *A Walk for Sunshine: a 2,160-mile Expedition for Charity on the Appalachian Trail*, New York City, NY: Beaufort Books Publishers, 2015.

Alt, Jeff. *Get Your Kids Hiking: How to Start Them Young and Keep it Fun!*, New York City, NY: Beaufort Books Publishers, 2013.

Avery, Myron, Maine: An Encyclopedia. Accessed October 4, 2015. http://maineanencyclopedia.com/myron-avery/

Badger, Robert L. *Geology Along Skyline Drive Shenandoah National Park, Virginia*, Shenandoah National Park Association, 2012.

Bove, Jennifer. Why does it Matter if Species go Extinct? About.com, December 10, 2014. Accessed December 28, 2015. http://endangeredspecies.about.com/od/extinctionpastandpresent/a/Why-Does-It-Matter-If-Species-Go-Extinct.htm

Davenport, Coral. Climate Change Deemed Growing Security Threat by Military Researchers, The New York Times, May 13, 2014. Accessed September 19, 2015. http://www.nytimes.com/2014/05/14/us/politics/climate-change-deemed-growing-security-threat-by-military-researchers.html

Davenport, Coral. Pentagon Signals Security Risks of Climate Change, New York Times, October 13, 2014. Accessed September 19, 2015. http://www.nytimes.com/2014/10/14/us/pentagon-says-global-warming-presents-immediate-security-threat.html?_r=0

Denker, Ellen P. Historic Furnishing Report, Massanutten Lodge at Skyland Shenandoah National Park, Luray Virginia, Northeast Museum Services

Center, National Park Service, Boston, MS, 2000. Accessed January 29, 2016.

Eisenfeld, Sue. *Shenandoah: A Story of Conservation and Betrayal.* Lincoln, NE: University of Nebraska Press, 2014

Engle, Reed L. *Everything Was Wonderful: A Pictorial History of the Civilian Conversation Corps in Shenandoah National Park,* Luray, VA: Shenandoah National Park Association, 1999

Engle, Reed L. *In the Light of the Mountain: An Illustrated History of Skyland,* Luray, VA: Shenandoah National Park Association, 2003.

Engle, Reed L. *The Greatest Single Feature...A Skyline Drive,* Luray, VA: Shenandoah National Park Association, 2006.

Engle, Reed E. and Darwin Lambert. *Herbert Hoover's Hideaway: The Story of President Hoover's Summer Retreat.* Luray, VA: Shenandoah National Park Association, 2011.

FDR Visits Foresters, Shenandoah National Park 1933/8/14, Universal News Reels. Accessed December 8, 2015. https://www.youtube.com/watch?v=3SdvYOHKyU4

United States.U.S. Fish and Wildlife Service. Accessed December 28, 2015. https://www.fws.gov/northeast/pdf/ShenandoahSalamander.pdf

Franklin D. Roosevelt, Gen. Malone, Howe, Ickes, Fechner, Wallace, and Tugwell in the Shenandoah Valley, Virginia, Franklin D. Roosevelt Library Digital Archives, August 12, 1933. http://www.fdrlibrary.marist.edu/daybyday/resource/august-1933-7/

Green, Kevin. Researcher: Salamanders are important to environment, The Northern Virginia Daily, December 15, 2014. Accessed December 28, 2015. http://www.nvdaily.com/news/2014/12/local-researcher-salamanders-something-to-look-after/

Hikes to Peaks & Vistas in Shenandoah National Park, Luray, VA: Shenandoah National Park Association, 2002.

Hikes to Waterfalls in Shenandoah National Park, Luray, VA: Shenandoah National Park Association, 2005.

Horning, Audrey. *On the Shadow of Ragged Mountain: Historical Archaeology of Nicholson, Corbin, & Weakley Hollows,* Luray, VA: Shenandoah National Park Association, 2004.

Iapetus Ocean, Wikipedia. Accessed November 19, 2015. https://en.wikipedia.org/wiki/Iapetus_Ocean

James, Phil. Secrets of the Blue Ridge: Rockfish Gap Through Afton Mountain, Crozette Gazette, November 5, 2012. Accessed May 22, 2015. http://www.crozetgazette.com/2012/11/secrets-of-the-blue-ridge-rockfish-gap-through-afton-mountain/

Janeczko, Paul B. and Jenna LaReau. *Top Secret: A Handbook of Codes, Ciphers, and Secret Writing,* Somerville, MA: Candlewick Press, 2004.

BIBLIOGRAPHY

Junior Ranger Explorer Notebook: Shenandoah National Park: Luray, VA: Shenandoah National Park Association, 1996

Kiger, Patrick J. "CIA Stops Sharing Climate Change Info With Scientists." Discovery News. May 26, 2015. Accessed January 4, 2016. http://news.discovery.com/earth/global-warming/cia-stops-sharing-climate-change-info-with-scientists-150526.htm

Lambert, Darwin. *The Undying Past of Shenandoah National Park*, Boulder, CO: Roberts Rinehart Publishers, 1989.

Lou Henry Hoover Biographical Sketch, Herbert Hoover Presidential Library Museum. Accessed January 17, 2016. http://www.hoover.archives.gov/info/LouBio.html

Lou Hoover Biography, National First Ladies Library. Accessed January 17, 2016. http://www.firstladies.org/biographies/firstladies.aspx?biography=32

Mapping the Appalachian Trail, How the AT was created ans surveyed, from Avery's wheel to GPS, xyHT, May, 2015. Accessed October 4, 2015. http://www.xyht.com/surveying/mapping-the-appalachian-trail/

Montell, William Lynwood. "People of the Shenandoah Valley" .Shenandoah Valley Folklife, pp3-14, Jackson MS. Univeristy of Mississippi Press, 1999

Mussulman, Joseph. "Jefferson's Cipher for Lewis." www.Lewis-Clark.org (date retrieved: January 29, 2014). http://www.lewis-clark.org/content/content-article.asp?ArticleID=2222

Neufeld, Howard S. Forests of a Century Ago – The Dominance of the American Chestnuts, Department of Biology, Appalachian State University, September 9, 2015. Accessed December 18, 2015. http://biology.appstate.edu/fall-colors/essays

Paleo-Indians in Virginia. Accessed June 1, 2015. http://www.virginiaplaces.org/nativeamerican/paleoindians.html

Pfanz, Don. Stonewall Marches Through the Shenandoah, The 1862 Shenandoah Campaign. Accessed October 12, 2015. http://www.civilwar.org/battlefields/portrepublic/port-republic-history-articles/pfanzshenandoah.html

United States. National Park Service. "President Herbert Hoover and Lou Henry Hoover's Rapidan Camp Virginia (U.S. National Park Service)." Accessed December 30, 2015. http://www.nps.gov/nr/travel/presidents/hoover_camp_rapidan.html

United States. National Park Service. "Shenandoah National Park (U.S. National Park Service)." National Park Service. Accessed April 27, 2015, May 10, 2015, June 27, 2015, October 18, 2015, November 7, November 8, 2015,2015, November 15, 2015, December 4, 2015, December 11, 2015, December 18, 2015, December 22, 2015, December 27, 2015, December 28, 2015, December 31, 2015, January 1, 2016, January 2, 2016, January 3, 2016, January 7, 2016, January 9, 2016, , http://www.nps.gov/shen/index.htm

United States. Potomac Appalachian Trail Club. Accessed September 5, 2015 & September 17, 2015. http://www.patc.net/Patc/

Reader, Carolyn and Jack. *Shenandoah Secrets: The Story of the Park's Hidden Past*, Vienna, VA: Potomac Appalachian Trail Club, 1991.

Reshetiloff, Kathy. Shenandoah salamander, a rare find, becoming even more scarce, Bay Journal, March 24, 2015. Accessed November 15, 2015. http://www.bayjournal.com/article/shenandoah_salamander_a_rare_find_becoming_even_more_scarce

Rockewell, Craig. "The Secret Code for Lewis & Clark." Lewisandclarktrail.com (Date retrieved: January 2014). http://www.lewisandclarktrail.com/legacy/secretcode.htm

Short Hikes in Shenandoah National Park, Luray, VA: Shenandoah National Park Association, 2010.

Stone, Dan. Saving Salamanders in Shenandoah, Smithsonian National Zoological Park, March-April, 2009. Accessed November 15, 2015. http://nationalzoo.si.edu/Publications/ZooGoer/2009/2/SavingSalamanders.cfm

Stoneberger, John W. *Memories of a Lewis Mountain Man*, Vienna, VA: Potomac Appalachian Trail Club, 1993.

Swenson, Ben. Far Pocosin, or, Pocosin Mission; Shenandoah National Park, January 7, 2013. Accessed December 13, 2015. http://www.abandonedcountry.com/2013/01/07/far-pocosan-wild-with-moonshine-whiskey/

Tabler, Dave. "Why Not Skyland." Appalachian History. July 2, 2013. Accessed January 8, 2016. http://www.appalachianhistory.net/2013/07/why-not-skyland.html

The American Chestnut Foundation. Accessed December 18, 2015. http://www.acf.org

The Avery Legacy, South Shenandoah. Accessed September 27, 2015. http://www.southshenandoah.net/the-patc/patc-history/myron-avery.html

The McGuffey Readers. Accessed December 15, 2015. http://www.mcguffeyreaders.com/1836_original.htm

Timeline of the Founding of the University of Virginia, Thomas Jefferson's Monticello. Accessed Janaury 10, 2016. https://www.monticello.org/site/research-and-collections/timeline-founding-university-virginia

Whisnant, Anne Mitchell, David E. Whisnant, and Tim Silver. Shenandoah National Park, Virginia Beach, VA: The Donning Company Publishers, 2011.

Wilson, Glynn. Climate Change Comes to Shenandoah, New American Journal, November 17, 2014. Accessed September 16, 2015. http://www.newamericanjournal.net/2014/11/climate-change-comes-to-shenandoah/

Wright, Lisa Regan. Wolly Mammoths roamed through Virginia during the Ice Age. July, 12, 2010. Accessed January 9th, 2016. http://articles.dailypress.com/2010-07-12/news/dp-fea-naturenotes-0711-20100710_1_mammoths-woolly-ice-age

BIBLIOGRAPHY

Non-Publication Sources

Deitzer, Bill. Lecture, January, 2016

Dickey Ridge Visitor Center, Shenandoah National Park, Front Royal, Virginia, May 2015

Evans, Meredith, Lecture, Park Ranger, Interpretation and Education Division, Dickey Ridge Visitor Center, Shenandoah National Park, Luray, Virginia, May, 2015

Harry F. Byrd, Sr. Visitor Center, Shenandoah National Park, Stanley Virginia, July, 2015

Hubert, Sally. E-mail correspondence, Park Ranger, Interpretation and Education Division, Shenandoah National Park, Luray, Virginia, February, 2015

King, Brian. E-mail correspondence, Publisher, Appalachian Trail Conservancy, June, 2015.

Massannutten Lodge, Skyland, Shenandoah National Park, Virginia, June, 2015

Rapidan Camp, Shenandoah National Park, Syria, Virginia, June, 2015

Rockfish Gap Tourist Information Center, Afton, Virginia, May, 2015

Selig, Lea, Lecture, Park Ranger, Interpretation and Education Division, Big Meadows Amphitheatre, Shenandoah National Park, Stanley, VA, July, 2015.

Wilcox, Jennifer, Lecture & e-mail correspondence, Museum Administrator/ Educational Coordinator, National Cryptologic Museum, National Security Agency, February 2015 & January, 2016.

ABOUT THE AUTHOR

Jeff Alt is an award-winning author, a talented speaker, and a family hiking and camping expert. Alt has been hiking since his youth. In addition to writing the *Adventures of Bubba Jones* book series, Alt is the author of *Four Boots-One Journey, Get Your Kids Hiking,* and *A Walk for Sunshine. A Walk for Sunshine* won the Gold in the 2009 Book of the Year awards sponsored by Fore Word Reviews; it took first place winner in the 2009 National Best Books Awards Sponsored by USA Book News, and won a Bronze in the 2010 Living Now Book Awards sponsored by Jenkins Group. *Get Your Kids Hiking* won the bronze in both the 2014 Living Now Book Awards and the 2013 IndieFab Award; in Family and Relationships. Alt is a member of the Outdoor Writers Association of America (OWAA). He has walked the Appalachian Trail, the John Muir Trail with his wife, and has carried his 21-month old daughter across a path in Ireland. Alt's son was on the Appalachian Trail at six weeks of age. Alt lives with his wife and two kids in Cincinnati, Ohio.

For more information about *The Adventures of Bubba Jones* visit: www.bubbajones.com. For more information about Jeff Alt visit: www.jeffalt.com.

E-mail the author: jeff@jeffalt.com.

MORE FROM THE BUBBA JONES SERIES

Great Smoky Mountains (2015)

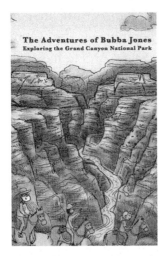

Grand Canyon (2018)

Acadia (2017)